Terrors out of Time

'. . . most people never quite know how much or how little they believe of matters ab-human or ab-normal, and generally they never have an opportunity to learn.'
    The Thing Invisible, William Hope Hodgson

Labyrinthine passages, guarded by ancient and unimaginable horrors, lie hidden beneath the sands of Egypt. You must tread these musty pathways, following your arch-enemy to the very foundations of time, in a desperate battle to save the universe from destruction. All your powers and knowledge as a psychic investigator will be tested to their limits in this dark and dangerous mystery. Who is the infamous Baron Ausbach and what are the evil masters he serves? Do you dare to follow him across Europe in search of the secrets of time? Will you be able to discover the hidden ways of the pyramid without losing your life or your sanity?

D1136760

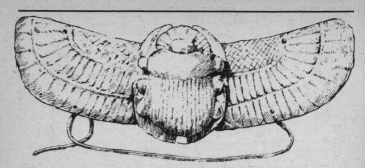

Forbidden Gateway
Book 2

Terrors out of Time

CLIVE and IAN BAILEY

Illustrated by Jonathan Heap

A Magnet Book

To Vivien
(for putting up with it)

Also available in Magnet Books:

Where the Shadows Stalk

About the Authors
Clive and Ian Bailey have a long association with
adventure games. Dedicated gamers since 1974, they
both joined Games Workshop in 1981 (where they
helped to select and launch Runequest) and they have
been involved in developing and marketing new
game: a simple but efficient and adaptable rules
fantasy role-playing magazines and organise games
conventions.

Both authors know the ingredients for a good
game: a simple, but efficient and adaptable rules
system, a coherent plot with plenty of variety and a
cracking pace – and lots of scope for the imagination.
Both authors also have a weakness for last century's
gothic horror stories, revealing the mysteries behind
the commonplace. One dark November night, with an
eerie wind whistling outside, they began to swop
weird tales and horrid imaginings – and the Forbidden
Gateway opened . . .

First published in Great Britain 1985
by Methuen Children's Books Ltd,
11 New Fetter Lane, London EC4P 4EE.
Text copyright © 1985 Clive and Ian Bailey.
Illustrations copyright © 1985 Jonathan Heap.
Printed in Great Britain by Richard Clay (The Chaucer Press) Ltd,
Bungay, Suffolk

British Library Cataloguing in Publication Data

Bailey, Clive
   Terrors out of time. – (Forbidden gateway; 2)
   – (A Magnet book)
   I. Title II. Bailey, Ian   III. Heap, Jonathan
   IV. Series
   823'.914[J]   PZ7

ISBN 0–416–52520–2

Forbidden Gateway

Terrors out of Time is your second adventure as a psychic investigator, dedicated to fighting the powers that lurk beyond the light of sanity and science. In **Where the Shadows Stalk** you travelled to the remote Welsh village of Bryn Coedwig to help your trusted friend and adviser, Charles Petrie-Smith, unravel a dark mystery. You became involved in a desperate battle against the forces of Outer Darkness, a battle which ended in your gaining possession of a curious crystal pyramidion. Neither you nor Petrie-Smith, for all his academic studies and research, have been able to discover anything about its origin or history. You take it back to London to examine it more closely in the comfort of your own home, unaware that the pyramidion is about to plunge you into another perilous encounter with the forces of evil.

In this adventure your decisions will affect the course of events for better or worse. In order to play your role to the full, you will need two six-sided dice (2D6), a pencil, rubber and a sheet of paper for any notes or maps you wish to make. A Character Profile sheet has been provided to help you keep track of your character's health and possessions throughout the adventure.

Before you can begin the adventure you must first generate a character to play with. If you have taken part in **Terrors out of Time**, you will already have a character. If not, follow the instructions below.

Generating your character

Investigators in **Terrors out of Time** require a number of special attributes. You will need one six-sided die (1D6) to generate these attributes and you are advised to record them on the Character Profile in pencil.

Strength: This is a measure of your physical power. Roll one six-sided die and add three to the score. Enter this figure in the box marked Strength on your Character Profile.

Stamina: This is a measure of your ability to sustain physical damage and is a product of your Strength. Multiply your Strength by two and enter the total in the box marked Stamina. If at any time during the course of the adventure your Stamina is reduced to zero or less, then your investigator will die. See the Insanity and Death section at the end of these rules.

Mentality: This is a measure of your intellectual ability and mental fortitude. Roll one six-sided die and add three to the score. Enter the total in the box marked Mentality.

Endurance: Endurance is a measure of your ability to withstand shock or mental stress. Multiply your Mentality by two and enter the score in the box marked Endurance. If at any time your Endurance is reduced to zero or less, your character will enter a state of severe shock and will be unable to continue the adventure. See the Insanity and Death section at the end of these rules.

Dexterity: This attribute measures your ability to handle mechanical devices, or to perform any actions requiring mental and physical co-ordination. Roll one six-sided die and add three to the score. Enter the score in the box marked Dexterity.

The Game System
During the course of the adventure, you will be required to perform tasks which test your attributes to

the full. To discover if you have completed a task you must roll two six-sided dice and compare the total to the rating of the attribute in question. If you have scored a sum that is equal to or less than the rating, then you will have succeeded. A score over the rating signifies you have failed and must follow the instructions that will be provided. This rule is the one that you will most commonly encounter.

Example:

238

Boldly, you climb upon the balcony rail, then launch yourself through space towards the chandelier. You hope your leap will carry you across the hall to where Ausbach stands. Roll against your Dexterity and if you succeed, turn to **251**. If you fail, turn to **278**.

Let us presume your investigator has a Dexterity of 7 and you roll a 4 and a 2 on the two dice. $4 + 2 = 6$, so you have rolled under your Dexterity and may turn to **251**. If you had rolled a $5 + 3 = 8$ you would have rolled over your Dexterity and been forced to follow the instruction to turn to **278**.

Combat

All the battles and encounters in this adventure have been programmed to provide you with a variety of choices and ease of play. Generally the rule above will cover most options in an encounter but occasionally, if you enter hand-to-hand or psychic conflict, you will be instructed to refer to the Conflict Table. This table is presented below and is repeated after your Character Profile.

Conflict Table

ATTACKER

	2	3	4	5	6	7	8	9	10	11	12
2	7	7	8	9	10	11	A	A	A	A	A
3	6	7	7	8	9	10	11	A	A	A	A
4	5	6	7	7	8	9	10	11	A	A	A
5	4	5	6	7	7	8	9	10	11	A	A
6	3	4	5	6	7	7	8	9	10	11	A
7	2	3	4	5	6	7	7	8	9	10	11
8	–	2	3	4	5	6	7	7	8	9	10
9	–	–	2	3	4	5	6	7	7	8	9
10	–	–	–	2	3	4	5	6	7	7	8
11	–	–	–	–	2	3	4	5	6	7	7
12	–	–	–	–	–	2	3	4	5	6	7

DEFENDER

NOTE
A = Automatic success
– = Automatic failure.

Example:

298

Desperately, you struggle to free yourself from the assassin-bug's embrace of death. Match your Strength against the creature's Strength (8) on the Conflict Table. If you fail, turn to **271**. If you succeed, will you use your pistol? Turn to **314**. Or, if your magazine is empty, will you engage in hand-to-hand combat? Turn to **352**.

Let us presume your investigator has a Strength of 7. As you are attempting to overcome the creature's Strength, look along the attacker's line of the Conflict Table. Then follow the column of numbers down until it crosses the defender's row marked 8 (the assassin-bug's Strength.) Where the two rows cross you will find a new rating of 6. It is against this number that you must now roll two six-sided dice. Roll under the number and you succeed. Roll over the number and you fail.

As a general guide, if you are stronger than your opponent the Conflict Table will increase your chance of success, but if you are weaker it will have the opposite effect.

Weapons and Artefacts

To kill or defeat creatures in **Terrors out of Time** you must either perform an heroic action, or reduce their Stamina or Endurance to zero. To reduce Stamina or Endurance, you need a weapon capable of damaging one or both of these attributes. You must also succeed in hitting your opponent with that weapon by rolling against your Strength or Dexterity, as the book requires.

If you look at your Character Profile, you will notice a section marked Combat, sub-headed Weapons. You begin **Terrors out of Time** in your own house, so you are considered to be unarmed apart from your fists. Your fists have been entered on the Character Profile and their damage factor of 2 has been entered in the STA column. This means they can inflict 2 points of damage on your opponent's Stamina (STA = Stamina; END = Endurance). You will acquire more weapons as you progress through the adventure and these should be entered on your Character Profile. A new weapon will be presented in the following style: Club 3/–. This means the club can inflict three points of Stamina damage but it cannot affect an enemy's Endurance. The position of the damage factor to the left or right of the dash denotes whether it affects an opponent's Stamina or Endurance, in that order.

During the course of the adventure you may also discover one or more artefacts – items which have the power to affect both you and your opponents. As a word of warning, artefacts are usually very powerful but they have a tendency to turn on their user, so they should always be used sparingly.

If you have read **Where the Shadows Stalk**, you may still possess the warrior's wand. You may use it in this adventure, whenever the text provides an option to cast it.

Finally, there is one general rule covering the use of weapons and those artefacts capable of inflicting damage. If you roll a double one on the dice, you score double the usual amount of damage with that blow. This rule represents good luck – and it applies to your enemies as well as you!

Insanity and Death

If your Endurance is reduced to zero or less, your character is presumed to have suffered such mental stress that he is no longer capable of continuing with his investigations. If your Stamina is reduced to zero or less, your character dies and the adventure ends.

To try and avoid such an occurrence, at the end of each day the book will instruct you to regain half of any lost Stamina or Endurance rounded down. To calculate this recovery, take your original Stamina rating and then subtract the current rating. Divide the resulting number by two and, dropping any fractions, add this final total back on to your current rating.

Example: If you start the adventure with a Stamina of 16 and lose 7 points during the first day, you will end up that night with a current Stamina of 9. Subtracting 9 from 16 leaves 7 and half of 7 is $3\frac{1}{2}$. Drop the fraction ($\frac{1}{2}$) and add the result of 3 back on to your current Stamina, giving it a new total of 12. At first glance, this calculation may seem a little confusing but it is really very simple and reflects our body's limited ability to recover from wounds through rest.

Exactly the same process is applied to calculate any Endurance recovery. Please note that recovery is always based on the difference between your original and current ratings. Consequently you can never end up with a rating higher than the one you started the game with.

If, despite the recovery rule you are killed (Stamina reduced to zero), or your mind snaps (Endurance reduced to zero) you will be instructed to turn to a death or insanity exit. **If no exit is offered, make use of either of the reference numbers printed on your Character Profile.**

Remember, if your character comes to an untimely end, simply roll up a new investigator and start again.

This is all you need to know to start investigating **Terrors out of Time**.

Good luck!

Investigator's Character Profile

NAME:

Attributes: Strength (STR)	Stamina (STA)
Mentality (MEN)	Endurance (END)
Dexterity (DEX)	If at any time the investigator's Stamina or Endurance are reduced to zero (0) and no exit is provided in the text, use the following entries: Stamina 250. Endurance 223.

Combat

WEAPONS	DAMAGE STA / END
Fists	2 / –

Possessions

REMEMBER:
When fighting, a roll of two ones on the dice indicates double damage. Deduct twice the amount of damage from the Stamina or Endurance of the creature you are fighting.

Encounters

Monster	STR	STA	MEN	END	DEX	DAM
1						
2						
3						
4						
5						
6						
7						
8						
9						
10						
11						
12						
13						
14						
15						
16						
17						
18						
19						
20						
21						

Conflict Table

ATTACKER

DEFENDER	2	3	4	5	6	7	8	9	10	11	12
2	7	7	8	9	10	11	A	A	A	A	A
3	6	7	7	8	9	10	11	A	A	A	A
4	5	6	7	7	8	9	10	11	A	A	A
5	4	5	6	7	7	8	9	10	11	A	A
6	3	4	5	6	7	7	8	9	10	11	A
7	2	3	4	5	6	7	7	8	9	10	11
8	–	2	3	4	5	6	7	7	8	9	10
9	–	–	2	3	4	5	6	7	7	8	9
10	–	–	–	2	3	4	5	6	7	7	8
11	–	–	–	–	2	3	4	5	6	7	7
12	–	–	–	–	–	2	3	4	5	6	7

NOTE
A = Automatic success
– = Automatic failure.

1

The wood around the door lock bulges, cracks and then splinters. Hinges creak and a pale hairless head emerges into the still night air. For a moment it pauses, grotesque ears listen for any sounds of alarm, then the figure of a painfully thin man squeezes out of the doorway.

Muttering to himself, he plunges down a deserted side street, where tendrils of dank unhealthy mist begin to curl from the sewer gratings as he passes. The man draws the tendrils around him like a thick cloak. Hidden from view, he pads silently towards the houses that surround the British Museum. Turn to **16**.

2

The sword point drives easily through the mummy's brittle wrappings, and on into the desiccated body. Finally, the point grates on the ancient spine. There is a searing blue flash and the sorcerous force which animated the ancient corpse discharges down the blade and into your body!

Match your Mentality against the power of the discharge (8) on the Conflict Table. If you succeed, turn to **12**. If you fail, turn to **131**.

3

At last your terrible wounds take effect. You sway, then your legs give way and you fall face down upon the floor. The hunchback grunts with satisfaction then kneels beside you.

As your mind slips into darkness you hear the creature mumble, 'My master will be pleased with me.' The adventure is over for you.

4

You lose 2 points of Endurance as the horror materialises before you. The creature leaps upon you and locks its talons about your neck! The oily black smoke cocoons you. You struggle to protect yourself, but your hands simply clutch at smoke! Now you feel a terrible pressure all over your body. Your skin begins to blister and crack. The horror is a succubus and it is sucking the moisture from your body!

Lose 3 points of Stamina. If this reduces you to zero, turn to **212**. If you still live, will you try to pipe upon the dragon whistle, if you have it? Turn to **91**. Or will you cast around for some other method of combating the creature? Turn to **152**.

5

With a yell, you struggle free from the creature's trance. (However, if your Mentality suffered in the struggle, it will remain reduced until you read recovery instructions.)

Now, how will you deal with this vile assassin? With your pistol, and risk blasting away vital controls? Turn to **70**. Or will you tear the fire extinguisher from its bracket and direct the contents over the beast? Turn to **112**.

To use the knobkerrie, roll against your Dexterity. Enter the following details on your Character Profile under Weapons: Knobkerrie 3/–. Each time you successfully strike a target, you will cause 3 points of damage to its Stamina.

If you are fighting the corpse-man thief, roll against your Dexterity. If you succeed, turn to **36**. If you fail, turn to **59**.

If you are fighting the mummy, turn to **135**.

'Well, let me think,' says the steward, scratching the back of his head. 'Several people came aboard in London, but only two are still here. An old invalid gentleman and his nurse in cabin 3 and an American gentleman in cabin 7. I am afraid I don't know their names. Still, you could always talk to the Purser, but watch him, he's a crabby old devil.'

Given the steward's scant information, will you visit the invalid's cabin? Turn to **192**. Will you investigate the American? Turn to **78**. Or will you interview the Purser? Turn to **33**.

In one fluid movement, you twist and block your attacker's dagger arm, then thrust your body backwards into him. The collision breaks the person's hold about your neck and throws him off balance. You turn, and confront the Baron's beautiful maidservant! The discovery is offputting. How can you strike this courageous woman, who is only defending the property of her master?

Hastily, you resolve to calm the maidservant, hoping to bluff your way from the cabin. As you contrive your explanation, she merely stares impassively at you, a stupid half-smile frozen on her lips. Perhaps she cannot understand English?

Suddenly, she cuts short your feeble account by lunging at you with the dagger. You dodge back, but the blade rips the arm of your jacket. Clearly, you must defend yourself from this plucky woman. (Note her Stamina (16) on your Character Profile.)

Will you cold-bloodedly level your pistol? Turn to **52**. Or will you try to wrest the dagger from her hand? Turn to **176**.

9

Match your Dexterity against the lock's complexity (7) on the Conflict Table. If you succeed, turn to **55**. If you fail, you must brave the window ledge. Turn to **37**.

10

Boldly, you step out around the pit's edge. Immediately, you sense a slight tremor in the ground and the grey light shimmers. A red aura suddenly boils up around the tree, then expands to fill the boundary of stones, bathing you in its weird glow. You see strange shapes forming on the tree's writhing branches like globular fruits. They resolve into the sad faces of long-dead men and women.

'Join us. Join us. Join us,' the faces call over and over again, in a terrible chant.

Roll against your Mentality. If you succeed, turn to **38**. If you fail, turn to **137**.

11

As you are about to descend the steps, you notice a thin wire that has been stretched across the entrance, about a foot from the floor. Gingerly stepping over it, you proceed with greater caution down the cramped and uneven steps. As you go deeper, dark stains begin to discolour the walls and the smell of herbs wafts up the stairwell. Then you round a corner and step into a room that is almost identical to the one you have just left. Turn to **53**.

12

The mummy sways, then slowly falls backwards off the sword tip. The ancient Egyptian collapses in a heap and acrid smoke begins to rise from its wrappings. You feel giddy from the discharge of energy you have endured and note your hand has been burnt (lose 1 point of Stamina).

However, the sound of alarm bells and shouting draws you from your stupor. It is time to flee from the devastation in the Egyptian room. Turn to **205**.

13

The hunchback cackles and a wash of foul breath splashes over your face. One of his legs is suddenly thrust up against your chest as he tries to break your grip and send you reeling across the kitchen. Match the hunchback's Strength (9) against your own Strength on the Conflict Table.

If he succeeds, you are thrown back across the room and suffer 1 point of damage to your Stamina when you collide with the kitchen table. Will you now draw your pistol and shoot the hunchback down? Turn to **66**. Or will you grab one of the candleholders as a weapon? Turn to **335**.

If he fails, match your Strength against the hunchback's Strength (9) on the Conflict Table. If you succeed, turn to **85**. If you fail, return and repeat this section again.

With consummate ease you evade the corpse-man's attack, drop under his guard and deftly skewer him. The thief lets out a thin scream and lurches backwards, clutching at his chest. He staggers to the sarcophagus, topples head first inside and disappears! You are alone in the museum. Turn to **99**.

Not quick enough! The dagger flashes past your arm, raised to block its downward plunge. Pain explodes through your shoulder. You have lost 3 points of Stamina.

Stung to action, you twist and grab your attacker's dagger arm, then thrust your body backwards into him. The collision breaks the person's hold about your neck and throws him off balance. You turn and confront the Baron's beautiful maidservant! The discovery is offputting. How can you strike this courageous woman, who is only defending the property of her master? Hastily, you resolve to calm the maidservant, hoping to bluff your way from the cabin. As you contrive your explanation she merely stares impassively at you, a stupid half-smile frozen on her lips. Perhaps she cannot understand English?

Suddenly, she cuts short your feeble account by lunging at you with the dagger. You dodge back, but the blade rips the arm of your jacket. Clearly, you must defend yourself from this plucky woman. (Note her Stamina (16) on your Character Profile.)

Will you level your pistol and open fire? Turn to **52**. Or will you try to wrest the dagger from her hand? Turn to **176**.

The pyramidion lies on your desk beside an open window as you gaze at it from the comfort of your armchair, wondering about its origins. Once again you consider its strange characteristics. Shaped like a miniature crystal pyramid, it is obviously of great antiquity. Its sides are unnaturally smooth and cannot be scratched, even by metal. Most puzzling of all is what is set inside the crystal: a stylised representation of a dragon, curling round to devour its own tail.

As you are lost in thought, a thin tendril of yellow mist comes over the sill and, with it, a wizened hand that feels its way across the desk top and seizes the crystal! With a shout, you bound to the window and look out. Your study is on the second floor, so you expect to see the thief on a ladder. Instead, crawling head first down the wall, is a thin man. You shout again and the thief leaps to the garden below. For a brief instant his hideous face leers up at you, then he turns and lopes away into the mist.

Snatching your coat from the back of a chair, you run for the door. How will you arm yourself? With the swordstick in the umbrella stand at the bottom of the stairs? Or with your trusty knobkerrie which lies against the wall? Select a weapon, note it on your Character Profile, then turn to **31**.

The khephera sword seems to be made of solid bronze, with a handle of gleaming white ivory. Presumably, it was used in some ancient rite, yet its edge is honed to a perfect sharpness and the whole thing is perfectly balanced. If you wish to take the sword, add this information to your Character Profile: Khephera Sword 5/–. Each time you strike with the sword, roll against your Dexterity. If you succeed, the sword will strike 5 points from an enemy's Stamina.

Will you now examine the crocodile cap? Turn to **41**. Or will you leave the chamber by a corridor in the far wall? Turn to **30**.

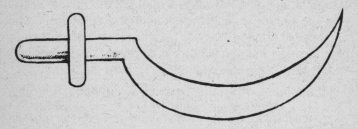

18

The creature's stupefying piping continues without pause, its legs swaying in time to the hellish beat. Match your Mentality against the creature's Mentality (7) on the Conflict Table. If you succeed, you break the creature's spell. Turn to **5**. If you fail, read on.

Your grip on reality is gradually slipping away. Deduct 1 point from your Mentality. Add this to the creature's Mentality. Now repeat the above section. Each time you fail to break the creature's spell, your mind will weaken and the creature's hold over you will increase. If your Mentality falls to zero, turn to **29**.

19

You awake to the sound of curtains being drawn. Confused, you gaze through bleary eyes around an unfamiliar room. Neat mahogany furniture and chrome fittings stare back.

A man dressed in white turns towards you and says, 'Good morning! It's nearly midday. I expect you would like some breakfast?' Then he smiles and leaves the room. At last, you are aboard the airship *Lucretia*.

During your sleep you have recovered half of any Stamina and Endurance lost during the events of last night.

If your Mentality was impaired, that has returned to its original value.

After breakfast, which restores a further 1 point of Stamina, the steward returns to collect your tray. Will you engage him in conversation about the passengers who boarded in London? Turn to **7**. Or dress and then interview the airship's Purser (the officer in charge of the airship's provisions and passenger welfare)? Turn to **33**.

20

The hunchback had an initial Stamina of 15. If the damage you have caused has reduced this figure to zero, turn to **184**. If the creature still lives, read on.

With a yell of fury, the hunchback swings the cleaver. Roll against his Dexterity (6). If he succeeds, you are wounded and lose 3 points of Stamina. If your Stamina is reduced to zero, turn to **3**. If not, read on.

You may fire one or two bullets, as you wish, but remember to roll each time for accuracy. Total the damage and deduct the bullets fired from your Character Profile. (If you have run out of bullets, you could fight on with the pistol's butt. Roll against your Dexterity. If you succeed, you cause 2 points of damage to the hunchback's Stamina.)

Now return to the first paragraph of this section. The battle proceeds in this way until either you or the hunchback is slain.

21

You need both your hands for the descent, so you are forced to make it in darkness. Extinguishing the lantern, you hang it from your belt and swing over the ledge. Then, clinging precariously to the holds, you begin the climb down. Roll against your Strength. If you succeed, turn to **327**. If you fail, turn to **340**.

22

To use the swordstick, roll against your Dexterity. Enter the following details on your Character Profile under Weapons: Swordstick 1D6/–. Each time you successfully skewer a target you will cause damage to its Stamina equivalent to the roll of one die (1D6).

If you are fighting the corpse-man thief, roll against your Dexterity. If you succeed, turn to **14**. If you fail, turn to **59**.

If you are fighting the mummy, turn to **353**.

23

Your gunfire blasts the creature back on to the steps of the Guardian's dais. It writhes for a moment, coughs and then lies still. You stride over the corpse and confront the Guardian. Turn to **77**.

24

You lose 1 point of Endurance as the horror materialises before you. It is an evil slavering succubus. You try to dodge past it, to flee from the room, but the thing moves with a horrible speed and blocks your escape.

Will you blast the thing with your automatic pistol? Turn to **35**. Cast the warrior's wand? Turn to **73**. Pipe upon the dragon whistle, if you have it? Turn to **91**. Or will you cast around for some other method of combating the creature? Turn to **152**.

25

You awake on a damp and musty four-poster bed. You have recovered none of the Stamina and Endurance lost during yesterday's encounters. With a start, you sit upright and stare in disbelief about an unfamiliar room. You seem to be in the circular chamber of a castle tower, yet it is furnished with objects from your airship cabin. All your possessions seem to be here too, strewn across the floor. A single doorway leads from the room, which is illuminated by light from a narrow open window.

You rise, gather your possessions, then investigate the door. It is locked. Turning to the window, you gaze out over the vista of a dark forest, which stretches away to the horizon. Below, is a sheer drop down the tower's flank to a rocky cliff and the silent waiting trees. A narrow crumbling ledge, a few feet below the window-sill, leads away around the side of the tower.

How will you escape from this room? If you have the skeleton key, you could pick the door lock. Turn to **9**. If you have lost the key, you must brave the window ledge. Turn to **37**.

26

Behind, you hear the sound of angry voices. The authorities have been roused by the night's events. Perhaps a well-aimed thrust to the mummy's shrivelled chest will deprive it of its unnatural life? Roll against your Dexterity. If you succeed, turn to **2**.

If you fail, the mummy attempts to ensnare you. Roll

against the corpse-creature's Dexterity (6). If it succeeds, turn to **280**. If it fails, you can fight on by repeating this section or attempt to dodge past the thing and escape, turn to **48**.

27

You lose 1 point of Endurance as you gaze through the serpent glass. You seem to be looking at a slowly opening door, from behind which emerges a beautiful maidservant. Stealthily, she enters an airship cabin and slips a curved ritual dagger from her coat. Her beautiful face is impassive as she tiptoes past a great oaken trunk . . .

The vision is suddenly interrupted. A floorboard creaks and you sense another person close behind you. Spinning round, you confront the beautiful maidservant. A horrid smile is clamped upon her face; the dagger is raised on high! Roll against your Dexterity. If you succeed, turn to **297**. If you fail, turn to **15**.

28

Cautiously, you hurry round the slimy wall of the pit. Nothing strange happens and you reach the entrance of another foul tunnel in safety. Turn to **197**.

29

Your body and mind have become numb, your legs sag and you collapse backwards on to the cabin floor. The assassin-bug leaves its perch and scuttles on to your chest.

You are dimly aware of its gloating cackle. 'Now, poor mortal, I shall feast on your brain!' The adventure is at an end.

30

The corridor is quite plain and terminates in a blank wall. If you are wearing the crocodile cap, turn to **51**. Otherwise you must make a Mentality roll. If you succeed, turn to **51**. If you fail, turn to **90**.

31

Taking the stairs two at a time, you rush to the street door, hurl back the bolts and plunge out into the sickly yellow mist. You pursue the thief up Bedford Terrace, below the imposing façade of the British Museum. On the corner of Bedford Square you pause. Silence. You have lost the burglar. Cursing, you are about to turn for home when you hear the groan of a door hinge. A brief investigation reveals that the back entrance to the museum has been forced. Stepping inside, you are rewarded by the sound of distant running footsteps from above.

There are two ascending stairways. Will you choose the one on your left? Turn to **54**. Or on your right? Turn to **76**.

32

As you are about to enter the stairwell, something snags your legs and you topple headlong down the stone steps!

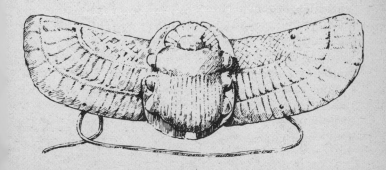

Lose 2 points of Stamina. If this reduces your Stamina to zero, your adventure ends here. Otherwise you land in a heap, bruised and battered, at the bottom of the steps. The lantern's glass is broken but, striking a match, you find the oil pan is still sealed and the wick will still burn. Lighting it, you find you are in a room which is almost identical to the one you have just left. Turn to **53**.

33

You find the airship's Purser seated at his desk in a tiny, but extremely neat, office. He is carefully entering figures into an accounts book. As you enter, he precisely applies a full stop to the last entry, before turning to greet you.

'May I help you?' he inquires in a tetchy voice. Remembering the airship receipt found at Shandwick House, you ask whether a Mr Ausbach is aboard.

The Purser raises his eyebrows above his pince-nez, sighs and draws a black leather-bound register from a drawer in his desk. He opens the cover and smooths the leaves with the back of his hand. A rather pudgy finger descends the passenger list, briefly pausing in two places. Then the Purser snaps the register shut and turns to you.

'Only two passengers remain from those who boarded in London: Baron Bachaus in cabin 3 and the celebrated American millionaire recluse, Colonel Hiram T. Schroeder, in cabin 7.'

Will you now resolve to visit the Baron? Turn to **192**. Or Colonel Hiram T. Schroeder? Turn to **78**.

Or will you see if you can extract any more information from the Purser? If this is your choice, match your Mentality against the Purser's Mentality (5) on the Conflict Table. If you fail, the purser refuses to give you any more information and you must choose one of the above options. If you succeed, turn to **371**.

34

You step from the kitchen's half-light into a very dark room. Switching on the torch, you illuminate a large wood-panelled dining-room. A great oak table, polished to a fine sheen, stands in the middle of the room, surrounded by ten dining-chairs. The windows are shuttered, the walls hung with moth-eaten hunting trophies and portraits of the Lathers family. By a door in the west wall you find a painting of Sir Roderick Lathers. He stands stiffly before the Egyptian Sphinx, a survey map in one hand and a pith helmet in the other. There is no similarity between this portrait and the ghoulish thief you encountered in the British Museum.

Quietly, you open the door and enter the gloom of a hallway. To your right, in a recess, stands a silent grandfather clock. To your left, the hallway stretches away into the silent house, apparently along its north–south axis. You proceed down the hall. Turn to **50**.

35

You fire once (deduct the bullet from your Character Profile), but the shot passes straight through the creature and crashes into the wall. Your attack seems to enrage the thing for it attacks again. Lose 3 points of Stamina. If this reduces your Stamina to zero, turn to **212**. If not, will you try to pipe upon the dragon whistle, if you have it? Turn to **91**. Or will you cast around for some other means of combating the creature? Turn to **152**.

36

Nimbly, you block the corpse-man's clumsy attack with the knobkerrie. Then, without a pause, you plunge the knobkerrie's gnarled butt-end down into the thief's ribs. He screams and lurches backwards, clutching at his chest.

He staggers to the sarcophagus, topples head first inside and disappears! You are alone in the museum. Turn to **99**.

37

Gingerly, you ease yourself out of the room and on to the ledge. A chill wind tugs at your clothes as your hands search for holds on the weather-beaten masonry. Hugging the wall, you begin to edge away from the window around the tower. You have taken but a few steps when a piece of the ledge, rotten with age, crumbles beneath your feet. Instantly, your fingers lock in their crevices. Desperately, your feet seek purchase on the sound part of the ledge. Roll against your Dexterity. If you succeed, you find a foothold and edge on round the tower to another window. Turn to **55**. If you fail, turn to **75**.

38

You have lost 1 point of Endurance. The terrible chant of the dead faces rolls on and on. A numbness creeps into your bones and you know the heads are chanting your very soul from your body. Vile images fill your mind. You see Ausbach and his minions casting people within the circle. Your breath comes in short agonised bursts and you know you must act, or risk death in the Well of Souls.

Match your Mentality against the Mentality of the soul tree (6). If you succeed, turn to **159**. If you fail, turn to **72**.

39

You gag at the vile sight, which has cost you 1 point of Endurance The pilot lies face up, half in and half out of his seat. His neck has been torn open and in his nerveless right hand a Luger pistol is still clutched. Did he kill himself?

Your answer comes in the form of a long and malevolent hiss. Out of the corner of your eye, you catch sight of a pair of giant spider-like legs, scrabbling for a hold on the co-pilot's seat. The hair on the nape of your neck begins to rise and a cold sweat breaks out upon your forehead. Turn to **86**.

40

You lose 1 point of Endurance as you look through the serpent glass. You gaze out across the ribbed top of the airship. A man stands upon the meteorological platform, his back bent into the wind. You cannot see his face, but there is something strangely familiar about his gaunt figure. His stance is like that of a conductor of a powerful symphony, but his disturbing jerky gestures are reminiscent of the corpse-man thief from the British Museum . . .

The mysterious vision is suddenly interrupted. A

floorboard creaks, a wickedly curved dagger glints and a sinuous arm clamps around your neck! Roll against your Dexterity. If you succeed, turn to **8**. If you fail, turn to **15**.

41

You pick up the crocodile cap, turning it over in your hands. It seems to be just a close-fitting skull cap, which may once have been used as a mark of rank or perhaps for a religious ceremony. Whilst you ponder on its use, a curious temptation to try it on creeps into your mind. Lifting it, you settle it over your head. Immediately, a sickening dizziness sweeps through your mind and you fall to your knees. Lose 1 point of Endurance.

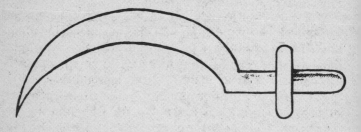

The sensation quickly passes and you rise feeling exhausted but at the same time oddly elated! Add the crocodile cap to your Character Profile. Will you now pick up the khephera sword? Turn to **17**. Or will you pass through the chamber to the corridor that pierces its far wall? Turn to **30**.

42

The sight of the thief's ghoulish features has cost you 1 point of Endurance. For an instant your guard drops and the corpse-man strikes! His abnormally long fingernails slash up towards your face.

Match the thief's Dexterity (8) against your Dexterity on the Conflict Table. If the thief is successful, turn to **59**. If he fails, you can retaliate with the swordstick, turn to **22**. Or the knobkerrie, turn to **6**.

43

You pull the lever and the wall before you sinks noiselessly into the ground. Before you lies a tunnel, its floor covered with dust and its walls decorated with scenes of ritual slaughter. Entering the tunnel, you watch the shadows flicker and flee before you, whilst behind you the dust billows up into the air. The tunnel leads you to a narrow ledge that juts out over a dark gulf. Lowering the lantern, you peer over the edge into darkness, but glancing to your right as you swing back, you notice a series of hand and foot holds that descend into the depths.

Will you try and use the holds to descend into this chasm? Turn to **21**. Or will you turn back to the chamber of the hieroglyphs, to explore the passage which leads to the Grand Gallery? Turn to **128**.

The hangar is full of freight: rows of bicycles wrapped in corrugated paper, a variety of passenger trunks and neat rows of wooden packing cases. You climb up among the cases and choose a safe hiding place and vantage point to await the airship's arrival.

Before long you hear the ponderous drone of aero engines. The *Lucretia* has arrived. As the airship manoeuvres her bulk over the docking beacon, you slip from your hiding place and join the throng of passengers and sightseers. Somewhere above lurks your quarry. Perhaps it is the corpse-man thief from the British Museum? Turn to **19**.

Returning to your cabin, you decide to keep watch on the mysterious Ausbach and Schroeder until the airship docks. At dinner there is no sign of your quarries, but you eat a hearty meal and recover 1 point of Stamina. Then you return to the cabin, where you fall into a deep slumber. Your dreams are strangely troubled by the odious images of the corpse-man from the British Museum and a horrible sensation of falling through the depths of the sky. Turn to **25**.

You turn to the journal's last entry, which was evidently written after Sir Roderick's return to England.

'I am sick of Ausbach and his meddling schemes. Today he returned from Wales in a vile brooding mood. After reading the morning's papers, he insisted that we include one of the sarcophagi in our bequest to the British Museum. However, later in the day, he made amends and gave me a fine painting of a seventeenth-century gentleman. I have hung the work over the mantelpiece in my room . . .'

You snap the journal shut and replace it in the bureau, then jump as something brushes against your shoulder. Turning, you see a tendril of oily smoke curling towards your throat. A strange indistinct terror is materialising before you. Roll against your Mentality. If you succeed, turn to **24**. If you fail, turn to **4**.

47

You step out into a strange bell-shaped pit. From far above, a thin grey light falls on seven great stumps of black stone, set in a circle. At their centre, stands the corpse of a long-dead tree; its twisted branches are loaded down with a moss which glows eerily in the half-light.

'We must be careful here,' Harold Lathers says. 'Ausbach calls this the Well of Souls. When I was first brought here, he threatened to cast me within the stone circle. We must keep close to the pit's edge. Come, there is another tunnel opposite us, behind the tree.'

Will you go left? Turn to **28**. Or right? Turn to **10**.

48

Can you dodge the mummy's clutches? Match your Dexterity against the mummy's Dexterity (6) on the Conflict Table. If you succeed, you dodge the clumsy corpse-creature. Turn to **205**. If you fail, you will be ensnared. Turn to **280**.

49

You have lost 2 points of Endurance.

The shrunken head hisses, 'I have come for you. Soon you will be in my power!'

The creature sits back upon six of its legs and raises the other two like a pair of batons. A strange, yet beguiling, piping issues forth from the creature's mouth. It fills the cabin and harmonises with the throb of the plane's engines.

The two legs tick fom side to side like a mad metronome. The creature is trying to hypnotise you. Turn to **18**.

50

As you silently pad along, your torch beam illuminates a procession of ornate plant holders, Grecian statuary and dingy still-life paintings. Presently, you come across an archway in the corridor's east wall, through which can be seen a spacious entrance hall. Will you investigate the entrance hall? Turn to **356**. Or will you return and open the last door you encountered? Turn to **333**.

51

The end wall is solid, but when you apply pressure to the wall on your right it swings out into another, far larger, corridor. As you step into this corridor, the wall swings to behind you. Looking to your right, you see that the passage disappears into darkness. On your left, it slopes down towards a yellow light. Could you have found Ausbach at last? Covering the lantern, you tiptoe down the corridor. Turn to **313**.

52

As the maidservant prepares for another lunge, you draw your pistol. You command her to throw down her dagger, or you will open fire. In response, the woman lowers her dagger hand. Taking this as a sign of acknowledgement, you back away towards the door. Yet, as your hand closes about the handle, the maidservant emits an extraordinary hissing sound, like that of an angered snake.

Roll against your Dexterity. If you succeed, you wrench the door open and escape into the corridor. There, you may choose to investigate the American's cabin. Turn to **78**. Or you may return to your own. Turn to **45**.

If you fail the roll, you flatten yourself against the door as the woman springs at you. You only have time to fire one or two bullets, remembering to roll against your Dexterity each time, for accuracy. Total the damage you have caused, strike the bullets fired from your Character Profile, then turn to **97**.

53

This room is also lined with red granite and contains another block of basalt. But behind the block looms an elaborately carved doorway, its flanks framed by interlocking snakes. Beside the block stands a trestle table, cluttered with bowls, phials and leather bags, from which rises the smell of herbs and spices.

Will you examine the items on the table? Turn to **92**. Or will you pass it by and hurry on through the carved doorway? Turn to **120**.

54

You clatter up the marble staircase and out into a dark deserted gallery. Squat Chinese statuary peers out at you from imposing display cases. Ahead, a doorway leads from the Chinese room.

You skid to a halt on the edge of a corridor and listen. Once again silence reigns. You must decide which way the fugitive went. Will you go left? Turn to **111**. Or right? Turn to **94**.

55

You step out on to a dark spiral staircase, which seems to lead down into the tower. Switching on your electric torch, you see that the walls run with damp. There is a smell of decay about this place. Now you begin a cautious descent, which is interrupted only by the discovery of a small room. Will you explore this room? Turn to **157**. Or will you descend further, to investigate the warm unpleasant breeze rising from below? Turn to **211**.

56

The interior of the temple is thick with an evil-smelling smoke that curls from a great fire in the centre of the floor. On either side the walls are lined with tiers of earthenware jars, encrusted with dust and sealed with clay representations of various beasts' heads. Beyond the fire is a low dais, a curious tripod and a high-backed chair, in which sits a wizened creature. As you skirt the fire, a dry

voice croaks from the seated figure.

'Greetings, mortal. I am the Guardian of the Dead. What brings the living to my hall?'

You tell him the ferryman said that you might learn some wisdom in this place and, at the same time, you ask after Ausbach.

'Wisdom! Yes, you may learn some wisdom,' chuckles the Guardian. 'Ausbach is a servitor and High Priest of Het. At this moment, he is both at the pit of time, summoning his mistress, and within these walls.'

As this riddle passes from the Guardian's cracked lips, he clicks his fingers and you hear the long-drawn howl of a mad dog. In the silence that follows, the Guardian points at you.

'Fool! I am not here to help you. I am here to destroy you! You are a trespasser and a meddler and your interference has already cost us valuable time – but now my creation will punish you!'

A crouching human figure rushes from the shadows to your left. It pauses and then growls at you. The creature is a man with a dog's head. Roll against your Mentality. If you succeed, turn to **294**. If you fail, turn to **283**.

57

The knobkerrie slices inexorably down. The swathed whimpering head explodes in a cloud of evil-smelling dust. Onward drives the knobkerrie, crushing the mummy's brittle chest. Then you are stunned by an enormous flash of blue light and the sorcerous energy, which animates the mummy, discharges along your weapon, splitting it from end to end. The corpse-creature's legs buckle and its ruined body slumps to the floor. The knobkerrie is now useless as a weapon. Delete it from your Character Profile.

You hear angry shouting from behind. The museum authorities have been roused by your intrusion. It is time to flee from the devastated Egyptian room. Turn to **205**.

58

Your blow shatters the creature's head and it collapses on the flagstones of the temple. With a triumphant grin, you turn on the Guardian of the Dead. Turn to **77**.

59

Sharp talons rake across your forehead, drawing blood. Then the corpse-man's body slams into you and you find yourself falling backwards, through a chaos of broken glass, beads and pottery shards.

As you struggle free from the smashed display case, you see your assailant turn, plunge head first into the sarcophagus, and disappear! You are alone in the museum. The wound to your forehead and the fall have cost you 1 point of Stamina. Turn to **99**.

60

You have lost 1 point of Endurance. Now, how will you deal with this vile assassin? Will you blast the creature with your gun, and risk shooting away vital controls? Turn to **70**. Or will you wrench the fire extinguisher from its bracket and direct the contents over the beast? Turn to **112**.

61

Carefully, you line the Junkers up for its landing and sweep in over the runway. The wheels touch the ground, the aircraft performs a spine-jarring bounce, but you are down! Easing back the throttles, you boldly roll towards the brightly-lit service hangars, bringing the aircraft to a halt next to an old biplane.

You cut the engines, scramble from your seat and jump from the fuselage door. There is no welcoming committee. Brazenly, you walk towards one of the hangars. Perhaps there you can find a safe hiding place to await the arrival of the airship *Lucretia*. The flight and the struggle with the assassin-bug have taken their toll: you are exhausted and have lost 1 point of Stamina. Turn to **44**.

Skipping on through the pages, you read:

'Everyone's spirits are low. First the sarcophagi were both found to be empty and now the lower passage, the Way of the Dead, has been found to terminate in an unfinished chamber. Ausbach is convinced there is a third chamber yet to be discovered, but whilst I agree with him, I find his continual mutterings about a fanciful key and his peculiar nocturnal habits more than I can bear . . .

'Ausbach has had a trestle table moved into the second chamber and spends most of the day inside the pyramid. The secondary excavations to the west have revealed nothing and now our funds, like our finds, are running low . . .

'Today, I entered the pyramid to tell Ausbach we must leave. As I neared the second chamber I heard strange mutterings, clicks and whistles and, fearing for his sanity, I rushed into the chamber. I found him hunched over a weird ball-shaped mirror and he glared up at me with a look of hatred and anger, but then his features softened and he slumped back in his chair. He took the news about the closure of the dig calmly, telling me he was glad, as he must travel immediately to Wales . . .'

Will you carry on reading the journal? Turn to **46**. Or will you investigate the bed? Turn to **361**.

63

Unable to fend off the entire bogie horde, you succumb to their sharp teeth and claws. As you fall beneath the slavering pack, your ears are filled with Harold Lathers' final screams. This adventure is over for you.

64

Taking a firm grip on your chosen weapon, you stealthily advance upon the man, who appears to be engrossed in some bizarre ritual. He mumbles in a strange and unknown language. It is ugly, cruel and rasping.

You halt a few feet from the thief and angrily announce, 'The game is up, my friend. Quit your vile blasphemies and turn around!'

The man's shoulders tense and an evil croaking laugh racks his body.

'Very well, my insistent friend,' he says. 'I will turn to face you.'

The thief turns towards you and, in the gloom of the museum, you stare into evil red-rimmed eyes, sense the dry flesh taut across the skull and glimpse a mouth too full of teeth.

Roll against your Mentality. If you succeed, turn to **42**. If you fail, turn to **71**.

65

You take the whistle from your mouth and turn to command the creature you have summoned. You gape into the maw of a mind-wrenching terror. Oily black smoke coils about the creature's fang-filled jaws. A myriad iridescent scales glitter in the night's gloom. Great feathered wings hold a horned and armoured body aloft. Cruel eyes regard both you and Ausbach. Then the beast belches and a plume of flame engulfs you; it gushes over Ausbach and ignites the fabric of the *Lucretia*'s hull. You perish in another unexplained airship disaster.

66

You tug the pistol from inside your jacket and blast the creature at point-blank range. A gout of lurid flame cuts through the gloom, illuminating the hunchback's contorted features. You may fire one or two bullets, as you wish, remembering to roll each time against your Dexterity for accuracy. Total the damage you have caused, deduct the number of shots fired from your Character Profile, then turn to **20**.

67

On the right leg a series of pictures show the mummification of Khefu's body; on the left leg his soul, in the guise of a human-headed bird, is shown leaving the mummy and flying from the pyramid. But the soul does not fly up into the sun. It flies across a dark pit and in its claws it carries a triangle that glows. Could this be a reference to the pyramidion? Looking closer, you see something has been inscribed on the triangle, but centuries of decay have blurred it beyond recognition. However, you do notice that the pit is filled with monstrous creatures, like great jelly-fish, that are beckoning to the triangle.

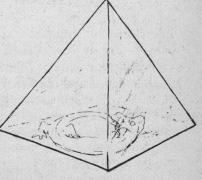

Will you now pass beneath the archway? Turn to **81**. Or will you retrace your steps to the chamber of the hieroglyphs, so you can explore the Way of the Dead? Turn to **146**.

68

You lose 1 point of Endurance as you look through the serpent glass. You gaze into a darkened room, in the middle of which stands a large man, dressed in an ill-fitting suit. He wears dark glasses and weaves strange signs in the air with his hands. Shadowy, unwholesome, fluttering things seem to be materialising about him . . .

This mysterious vision is suddenly interrupted. A floorboard creaks, a wickedly curved dagger glints and a sinuous arm clamps around your neck! Roll against your Dexterity. If you succeed, turn to **8**. If you fail, turn to **15**.

69

Your weapon slices neatly through the terracotta scorpion's sting. The effect is instant and quite startling. The creature begins to run amok, charging erratically into the other statues which litter the cavern floor. Its legs shatter and its claws break off. Finally, the hulk of the monster collapses in a cloud of dust.

You turn away and search for an exit from the cavern. Finding a cleft in the cavern wall, you scramble up and squeeze through the narrow gap. Turn to **130**.

70

You draw your pistol and point it at the creature.

'You fool!' it hisses. 'You cannot slay me with such a puny weapon. Submit to me.'

Will you believe the creature and grab the fire extinguisher instead? Turn to **121**.

Or will you resolve to blast the creature anyway? You may fire one, two or three bullets as you wish, remembering to roll against your Dexterity for accuracy. Total the damage you have caused and deduct the number of bullets fired from your Character Profile. Whatever happens, turn to **210**.

You are stunned by the sight of the thief's ghoulish features and lose 2 points of Endurance. The corpse-man takes immediate advantage of your shock and springs at you, attempting to slash your face with his abnormally long fingernails.

Roll against the corpse-man's Dexterity (8). If he succeeds, you suffer a wound to your forehead and 1 point loss to your Stamina. Then his body slams into you and you find yourself falling backwards through a chaos of broken glass, beads and pottery shards.

As you struggle from the smashed display case, you see your assailant turn, plunge head first into the sarcophagus, and disappear! You are alone in the museum. The fall through the display case has cost you a 1 point loss to your Stamina. Turn to **99.**

You have answered the soul tree's call and taken a step towards the edge of the stone circle (reduce your Mentality by 1). The tree senses your weakness and increases its vile chanting. Match your weakened Mentality against the soul tree's increased Mentality (7) on the Conflict Table. If you succeed, turn to **159**. If you fail, turn to **93**.

73

Desperately, you tug the wand from your pocket and lob it above the monster. For a brief instant the wand blazes like a burning torch, then disappears. You have lost 1 point of Endurance. Thunder crashes and a howling wind suddenly tears at the windows, which groan, then burst inward. Spectral corpse-hounds swarm into the room and set upon the horror! The succubus releases its grip about your neck to battle with the hounds, and you stagger from the room. Later, will you open the double doors on the landing? Turn to **325**. Or explore the north hallway? Turn to **245**.

74

You evade the creature's fumbling clutches and raise your knobkerrie for a new blow. Roll against your Dexterity. If you succeed, deduct the damage from the mummy's Stamina (6).

Now the mummy attempts to grab you. Roll against the corpse-creature's Dexterity. If the creature succeeds, turn to **280**. If it fails, you can fight on by repeating this section. If the mummy's Stamina is reduced to zero, turn to **96**. Or you can attempt to flee from this battle and the museum, turn to **48**.

75

Your arms are aching under the strain. Suddenly, your right hand slips from its precarious hold and you slither down the wall. Can you grab the ledge before you fall away to your doom? Roll against your Dexterity. If you succeed, turn to **98**. If you fail, turn to **134**.

76

Rapidly you climb the marble stairway and emerge into a dark deserted gallery. As you hurry through, you note that the imposing display cabinets present a variety of Chinese porcelain and statuary. Ahead, a doorway leads from the Chinese room.

You skid to a halt on the edge of a corridor and listen. Once again silence reigns. You must decide which way the fugitive went. Will you go left? Turn to **111**. Or right? Turn to **94**.

77

The wizened Guardian has left the chair and now cowers behind its back.

'Don't harm me, mortal,' he gibbers. 'If I die here, my soul will be consigned to the horrors of the Outer Darkness. I will answer any question you put to me.'

Grabbing the rags which cloak the creature's emaciated body, you demand an answer to his riddle. For how can Ausbach be in two places at the same time? The Guardian points towards the jars which line the hall.

'There, on the third shelf. Ausbach's life is within the pot, bound there by his mistress Het. Destroy the contents and you will destroy Ausbach at the same time!'

Flinging the Guardian to the floor, you stalk across the temple to the shelf. There lies a jar whose lid is fashioned into a perfect bust of Ausbach's odious features. Tearing off the lid, you dip your hand inside and draw out a brain that shudders in your hand! Lose 1 point of Endurance. Dropping it back into the jar, you take the pot from the shelf and march out of the temple for the pit of time. Turn to **269**.

78

You proceed directly to cabin 7 and place your ear to the door. No sounds reach you from within. What will you do now? Boldly rap upon the door? Turn to **116**. Or attempt to pick the lock with the skeleton key, if you have it? Turn to **145**.

79

Deftly, you dodge the terracotta scorpion's lumbering charge, then swing your weapon like a club in an effort to smash the creature's sting from its body. Roll against your Dexterity. If you succeed, turn to **69**.

If you fail, the creature attempts to scuttle round to face you. Match the scorpion's Dexterity (8) against your own Dexterity on the Conflict Table. If it succeeds, the creature will try to follow up its advantage and seize you in its claws. Roll against its Dexterity. If it succeeds, turn to **173**. If the creature fails, will you try to use the knobkerrie or swordstick again? Turn to **231**. Will you draw your pistol? Turn to **264**. Or will you pipe upon the dragon whistle? Turn to **200**.

80

You draw back the heavy velvet curtains and discover someone lying in the bed! Without thinking, you shine the torch full into the figure's face and recoil in horror. Roll against your Mentality. If you fail, lose 2 points of Endurance.

The body is horribly contorted. Skeletal hands clutch the blankets as if the person had died of fright. The skin of the face is stretched across the skull like parchment. The blackened lips curl back from the teeth in a terrible grin. If you examined the portrait in the dining-room, you may notice the corpse's resemblance to Sir Roderick Lathers. When you have recovered your composure will you go to the bureau? Turn to **361**. Or leave the room, either to open the double doors? Turn to **325**. Or to explore the north hallway? Turn to **245**.

81

Beyond the arch is a room lined with red granite. A large block of basalt, which once supported the sarcophagus of Khefu, fills the centre of the chamber. Behind it stands a gilded statue of the god Horus. The statue guards a narrow entrance in the far wall, through which you can see a crumbling flight of steps descending precipitously into darkness. Passing the block, you notice a ring of sand on its surface where someone has put a bag down and then picked it up again. Could Ausbach have come this way?

A sense of foreboding fills your mind. If you wish to descend the steps, you must make a Mentality roll. If you succeed, turn to **11**. If you fail, turn to **32**. If you would rather retrace your steps to the chamber of the hieroglyphs and explore the Way of the Dead, turn to **146**.

82

Desperately, you charge the mummy. Perhaps you can knock it to the ground and escape? Match your Strength against the mummy's sorcerous Strength (8) on the Conflict Table. If you succeed, the creature is propelled backwards through one of the glass display cases. You escape through one of the room's exits, turn to **205**.

If you fail, the mummy will attempt to ensnare you. Roll against the mummy's Dexterity (6). If the creature succeeds, you are ensnared, turn to **280**. If the mummy fails, you can try to escape again by returning to the beginning of this section.

83

As the last of the bogies succumbs to the sword's bloody blade, you push Harold through an archway and slam the door. Luckily, the bolt is on your side. For a few moments you recover your breath, then you head off along a dank corridor, lit by guttering reed torches. The way leads to the edge of a vast gloomy pit. Turn to **47**.

84

The object is like the rattle or comforter of some monstrous baby. A writhing serpent, fashioned from gold and silver, supports a crystal globe. You pick the thing up and glimpse grey indeterminate shapes floating within the globe. Who are you thinking of? The American? Turn to **68**. Baron von Ausbach? Turn to **40**. Or the Baron's beautiful maidservant? Turn to **27**.

85

You slam the hunchback's cleaver hand back against the wall. He grunts with pain and the savage weapon clatters to the floor. This loss seems to enrage the creature. First he kicks you in the shin, then barges you back across the room on to the table. You have lost 1 point of Stamina. (If your Stamina is reduced to zero, turn to **3**.) As you struggle to your feet, you see your opponent retrieve his cleaver and turn towards you.

Will you now draw your pistol and shoot the hunchback down? Turn to **66**. Or will you grab one of the candleholders as a weapon? Turn to **335**.

86

A creature resembling a giant spider with a humanoid head drags itself on to the co-pilot's seat. Its legs bristle with thick hairs and support a leathery bag-like body, covered with bright orange blotches. Malevolent eyes regard you out of the shrunken human head. With a horrible precision, the creature scuttles sideways on to the dead pilot's chest. A high-pitched cackle breaks forth from its fang-filled mouth.

You have encountered an assassin-bug, a creature drawn from the supernatural world to destroy you. It has a Stamina of 16. Note this on your Character Profile, then roll against your Mentality. If you succeed, turn to **60**. If you fail, turn to **49**.

'You see,' says Colonel Schroeder, 'Baron Ausbach is the very same fellow you apprehended in the British Museum. He was certain you would not survive an encounter with the assassin-bug aboard the mailplane. I rather hoped you would, for I see in you the persistence and courage, which are the fundamental requirements of investigators into the abhuman and abnormal. Ausbach is inclined to liquidate you, but I am inclined to initiate you into a partial knowledge of the dark forces upon which you have stumbled.'

Now that you have confirmed who the thief of the pyramidion is, will you cut short this interview with a deluded old man and make for Ausbach's cabin? Turn to **192**. Will you return to your own cabin? Turn to **45**. Or do you dare to hear more of your host's arcane lore? Turn to **336**.

With all your might, you play on upon the dragon whistle. Sweat breaks out across your forehead. You feel, too, a wave of sadness, a sense of loss, as if part of yourself is being sucked away as you play. You have lost 1 point of Endurance.

Ausbach staggers backwards against the handrail, his arms upraised in a gesture of defence. For the first time you see a look of fear grip his repellent features. A great gush of hot air rushes over you and you are thrust down on to the wooden walkway. As you struggle to your feet, you hear Ausbach scream and glimpse him struggling in the talons of some enormous beast.

A myriad iridescent scales glitter in the night's gloom. Thick, oily, black smoke wreathes the creature's horned and armoured body. Great feathered wings bear the beast and Ausbach up and away from the *Lucretia*. Yet you play

on, piping the creature back to its own diabolical dimension. Its passing is marked by a clap of thunder and a final gush of hot air. You are alone atop the *Lucretia*.

Returning to your cabin, you climb wearily into bed. For a long while you lie in the dark, pondering your final encounter with Ausbach, a sorcerer in the twentieth century. Then you fall into a deep slumber which is strangely troubled by Ausbach's odious features and a sensation of falling through the depths of the sky. Turn to **25**.

89

You circle above Munich and pick out the aerodrome. A green flare arcs into the night sky. Can you bring the heavy Junkers down safely? Match your Dexterity against the aircraft's controls (7) on the Conflict Table. If you succeed, turn to **61**. If you fail, turn to **101**.

90

You can find no secret exit from this corridor and, despondently, you turn back. You must now retrace your steps to the chamber of the hieroglyphs to explore the passage which leads to the Grand Gallery. Turn to **128**. If you have been poisoned by the scorpion, this journey will entail the loss of 4 points of Stamina. If this loss reduces your Stamina to zero, then your adventure ends here, as you collapse in the passages beneath the pyramid of Khefu.

91

Desperately, you tug the dragon whistle from your pocket and begin to pipe. No sound escapes from the instrument, but the porcelain jug which sits upon the wash-stand begins to rattle, and the succubus releases its grip about your neck.

An unnatural warm wind begins to beat into the room and you hear a far off flapping sound. With every second that you pipe, this sound of far off wings grows louder until the room reverberates with the pulsing thunderous sound. Will you continue to pipe upon the infernal whistle? Turn to **114**. Or will you cease and command whatever you have summoned? Turn to **141**.

92

Clearing a space for your lantern, you sift through the objects before you. The leather pouches and phials are empty and the bowls contain the residue of various sweet-smelling oils. Then you discover a leather bag which is still unopened. It contains something large and heavy. Gingerly, you loosen the twine round its neck, tip it up and shake out the contents.

To your horror, a severed human hand flops on to the table! It quivers with life, flexes its fingers and then crawls towards you like a tarantula. This is a legendary Hand of Glory, used by necromancers to destroy their enemies. Roll against your Mentality. If you succeed, turn to **158**. If you fail, turn to **188**.

93

You have taken yet another step towards the circle of stones. One more and you will cross the threshold and go to your doom (reduce your Mentality again by 1 point). Once again the tree increases the power of its chant. Now match your weakened Mentality against the soul tree's increased Mentality (8) on the Conflict Table. If you succeed, turn to **159**. If you fail, turn to **113**.

94

You hurry along the corridor, rattling the handles of a variety of locked doors which appear to lead into an administrative area. Finally, you turn a corner and find yourself before a large window. Dead end. Realising your mistake, you hasten back into the museum, past the Chinese gallery and on towards another doorway. Turn to **111**.

95

As you explore the south side of Shandwick House you discover a side door, hidden among the overgrown shrubbery. Pushing in among the foliage, you stealthily test the door handle. The door is locked.

You will have to make use of your skeleton key. Match your Dexterity against the door lock's complexity (8) on the Conflict Table. If you succeed, turn to **119**. If you fail, you will have to walk on around the house. Turn to **320**.

96

Finally, your battering takes effect. For a moment, the mummy sways in front of you, then its legs buckle and the corpse crashes to the floor. The long-dead Egyptian lets out one final rasping sigh before falling silent. An acrid smoke begins to rise from its wrappings.

Angry shouting from somewhere in the museum spurs you to action. The museum authorities have been roused by your intrusion. It is time to flee the devastation in the Egyptian room. Turn to **205**.

97

The sound of gunfire crashes through the cabin. If the damage you have caused reduces the maidservant's Stamina to zero, turn to **117**. If not, read on.

With a hiss of fury, the maidservant hurls herself upon you, slamming your body back against the door. Roll against her Dexterity (9). If she succeeds, her dagger slashes 2 points from your Stamina. If you are reduced to zero, turn to **317**.

If her attack fails, you could try to wrest the dagger from her grip. Turn to **176**. Or, if you still have bullets, fire again. If you choose this option, you may fire one or two bullets as you wish. Remember to roll against your Dexterity, for accuracy, each time you fire. Deduct the number of bullets used from your Character Profile, calculate the damage you have caused, then return to the start of this section.

98

You grab the edge of the ledge, throw one leg over the lip and finally drag your body up to safety. For a long while you lie in the cold wind, poised above the abyss. This ordeal has cost you 1 point of Stamina. After a while, you claw yourself upright and complete your circuit of the tower. Here you find another open window. Turn to **55**.

99

You approach the display case in which stands the mysterious sarcophagus. The door stands open and the lid of the sarcophagus has been placed on the floor. It, too,

bears the symbol of a serpent devouring its tail – just like the stolen pyramidion!

Stepping inside the display case, you swiftly examine the interior. There is no sign of a trapdoor, broken glass or false bottom to the sarcophagus. How can the corpse-man have vanished?

Will you investigate further? Turn to **118**. Or will you leave the museum before you are apprehended by the museum authorities? Turn to **205**.

100

Your gunfire smashes into the brittle creature. Its body disintegrates and the monstrosity collapses in a choking cloud of red dust. You turn to search for an exit from the cavern. Finding a narrow cleft in the wall, you scramble up and squeeze through the gap. Turn to **130**.

101

As you sweep into land, a red warning flare climbs into the night sky. The wheels touch the ground, the aircraft performs a spine-jarring bounce and you are down.

Suddenly, a row of parked aircraft loom out of the darkness! Desperately, you apply the brakes and pull back the engines' throttles. The plane slews off the runway and rolls on to the wet grass. One wheel digs into the soil, locks, and the plane's nose tips forward, flinging you up and out of your seat like a rag doll. Your head strikes the bulkhead and you lose consciousness. Turn to **136**.

102

You stumble backwards in horror. This vile sight has cost you 2 points of Endurance. The pilot lies face up, half in and half out of his seat. His neck has been torn open and a Luger pistol is gripped in the dead fingers of his right hand. Did he kill himself?

Your answer comes in the form of a long and malevolent

hiss. Out of the corner of your eye, you catch sight of a pair of giant spider-like legs, scrabbling for a hold on the co-pilot's seat. The hair on the nape of your neck begins to rise and a cold sweat breaks out upon your forehead. Turn to **86**.

103

Playing the lantern's light across the mural, you pick out the faint outlines of two outlandish figures concealed beneath the dark paint on the left-hand side. You scratch the paint and it begins to peel away, revealing a heavily muscled god with the head of a pig and a goddess with the head of a snake. They stand in opposition to Thoth and Anubis.

The hog-headed god points to the floor with a black staff. Following an imaginary line from its tip, you discover a cleverly concealed stone slab near the foot of the wall. You brush away the sand and dust and prise the stone loose. Underneath is a crude hollow and a metal lever.

Will you pull the lever? Turn to **43**. Or will you retrace your steps, to explore the Grand Gallery? Turn to **128**.

104

The bureau stands half-open. Inside are pens, paper and a ready supply of ink. There is also a journal, tied shut with a ribbon of red silk. The goldleafed title is *Excavation of the Pyramid of Khefu*. You undo the ribbon and briefly peruse the journal's pages. The majority of the account is typed but the last sections are completed in a bold longhand. Scanning the entries you deduce the following information:

'Today we cleared the Grand Gallery, but before entering the king's chamber, Ausbach insisted I order all the labourers out. Together we broke into the chamber and found the great sarcophagus of Khefu, resting upon a huge block of basalt. Ausbach was quite unimpressed by this find, instead he spent much time examining a statue of

Horus which stands against the chamber's rear wall . . .

'As I examined the hieroglyphs painted on Khefu's sarcophagus, there was an extraordinary gust of hot dry air, which almost extinguished my lantern. Turning, I saw Ausbach disappear through a doorway which had appeared in the side of the chamber! Coaxing my lantern back to life, I pursued the impetuous Baron into another chamber, which he seemed to be examining in the pitch dark! Here, to my amazement, was a second sarcophagus, identical in every respect to that in the upper chamber. There was also another passage leading off into the depths of the pyramid . . .'

Will you continue to read Sir Roderick's account? Turn to **62**. Or turn and examine the bed? Turn to **361**.

105

The mummy's convulsions wrench the swordstick from your hand. You are disarmed! The corpse-creature seems to sense this, for it begins to grope purposefully towards you once again.

Now you hear the sound of shouting from somewhere in the museum. The authorities have been roused by your intrusion. Will you fight on unarmed? Turn to **82**. Or will you attempt to evade the mummy's clutches and escape the devastated Egyptian room? Turn to **48**.

106

The creatures cough and choke as the corpse dust boils up around them. It seems to churn with a sinister life of its own, like a swarm of bees. The bogies crash to the floor and their bodies crumble into grey dust. The rest of the horde waver. You take advantage of this lull in the battle to drag Harold Lathers through the archway and slam the door. Luckily, the bolt is on your side. For a few moments you recover your breath, then you head off along a dark corridor lit by guttering reed torches. The way leads to the edge of a vast gloomy pit. Turn to **47**.

107

At the last moment you duck under the descending blade and blunder into the hunchback. The cleaver hurtles into the table top and locks into the wood. The half-man grunts with rage and violently cuffs you aside, causing 1 point of damage to your Stamina.

As the hunchback tries desperately to tug his weapon free, you aim a blow at his head. Roll against your Dexterity. If you succeed, you cause 2 points damage to his Stamina (15). If you fail, your puny blow merely enrages the creature. Whatever happens, turn to **209**.

108

While Ausbach continues his vile incantation, you slip the dragon whistle from your pocket, place it to your lips and begin to blow. No sound blares forth and, at first, nothing seems to happen. Then the savage storm wind begins to slacken, to be replaced by a new and unnatural warm wind.

Ausbach is clearly surprised by this strange turn in events. His incantation falters, the inhuman light dies in his eyes and he stands slack-shouldered before you.

'What sorcery can quell the wind lord's passion?' he cries. 'What magic have you squandered to aid you, meddling fool?'

As if in answer, you hear the beat of powerful wings and sense the presence of some monstrous terror. It is behind

you. It awaits your command. Will you continue to pipe upon the dragon whistle? Turn to **88**. Or will you cease playing and turn to command the beast? Turn to **65**.

109

Before you can catch your breath, the smoke engulfs you. Your throat burns, your eyes fill with tears and you choke. Desperately, you stagger towards the door, but your legs give way and you fall heavily. The choking sensation leaves you and you feel instead a great lethargy and sense your mind slipping towards oblivion. Your last memory is of a shadowy figure looming above you. It bends towards you and the ghoulish features of the British Museum corpse-man come into focus.

A heavily accented voice whispers in your ear, 'Your adventures are over. At last I am rid of your amateur meddling!'

110

The scorpion's sting smashes into your back and hurls you against the rock face. A burning pain fills your body. The scorpion turns away and scuttles off across the cavern.

You have been injected with a creeping poison and, until you discover a cure, you will lose 1 point of Stamina every time you turn to an odd-numbered section in this adventure. Note this on your Character Profile.

Shaking, you stagger to your feet and painfully squeeze through the cleft. Turn to **130**.

111

Before you stands an imposing columned doorway. A sign in large gold letters declares: Egyptian Rooms. You pass through the doorway and step into a lofty darkness. Great statues and strange mythological creatures loom before you.

You detect furtive movements ahead and realise that you are close to your quarry. Cautiously, you advance to the edge of a smaller gallery which is stuffed with glass cases of Egyptian funerary relics, sarcophagi and mummies. The thief, his back towards you, is busy before an open display case, in which stands a coffin-shaped sarcophagus.

Can you creep forward and surprise the man? Roll against your Dexterity. If you succeed, turn to **64**. If you fail, turn to **127**.

112

As you tear the fire extinguisher from the bulkhead, the creature screams, 'Submit to me!'

Coolly, you pull the extinguisher's safety pin and punch the fire button. A cloud of freezing carbon dioxide gas spurts forth from the extinguisher's nozzle. What effect will this improvised weapon have upon the monster? Roll 1 die and turn to the relevant entry:

    1–2 = **149**
      3 = **195**
    4–6 = **170**

113

Your mind has fallen under the soul tree's spell. Like a zombie, you step within the stone circle. Immediately, you sense an extreme heat and an instant later your body is consumed in a blaze of burning red light. Your soul remains to serve the vile schemes and dastardly magic of Baron Ausbach. This adventure is over for you.

114

On and on you pipe upon the infernal whistle. The succubus seems to waver, to shrink back towards the curious painting above the mantelpiece, which now glows with a baleful red light. Suddenly, a great gout of hot air rushes past you, hurling you down upon the floor. When you struggle to your feet, the horror has vanished and the room is once again chill and silent, but the picture is blackened and charred. You have lost 1 point of Endurance during the piping.

Shaken by your experience, you pocket the whistle and retreat from the room. Will you now try opening the double doors on the landing? Turn to **325**. Or will you explore the north hallway? Turn to **245**.

115

You awake to the sound of a key rattling in a door lock. The cell door swings open and a burly police sergeant steps inside.

'I've brought you some tea and a newspaper. Your little escapade has made the front pages!'

Your gaze falls upon the folded newspaper the sergeant hands you. The headline declares: 'Desecration of British Museum! Person helps police with inquiries. Charges pending.' You sigh, this adventure is over.

116

Your sharp knock is immediately answered by a rather irritable voice from within. 'Come in! Come in! It's not locked.' Turn to **296**.

117

The maidservant is caught by the impact of your fire and flung backwards against the great trunk. Slowly, she slumps to the floor. The dagger slips from her hand and she lies still, like a crumpled rag doll. Even in death, she smiles.

Sadly, you approach the corpse and survey your bloody work. Your eye is immediately caught by a peculiar green liquid oozing from the maidservant's hair. You crouch by the body and see that the woman's face is in fact a waxen mask. You tear the beautiful effigy aside and reveal a macabre secret: the maidservant is a serpent man! Green blood trickles from the creature's snout. Its red forked tongue lolls at one side of its fang-filled jaws. Dead yellow eyes stare accusingly. Roll against your Mentality. If you fail, lose 1 point of Endurance.

Fighting back a wave of nausea, you rise and leave Baron Ausbach's cabin. If you examined the serpent glass, you may choose to take it with you. Add it to your Character Profile under Possessions. Turn to **338**.

118

The sarcophagus itself is quite empty, but its bottom glistens like tar. Using your weapon as a probe, you prod the base. To your surprise, the surface gives like a sheet of rubber.

Match your Strength against the membrane's Strength (5) on the Conflict Table. If you are successful, turn to **133**. If you fail, turn to **190**.

119

Deftly, you manoeuvre the skeleton key about the old and apparently rusty lock. After a while your persistence is rewarded and you feel the lock grind back. The door creaks open to reveal a gloomy passageway, which seems to run along the north–south axis of the house. Shutting the door, you switch on the torch and play the beam briefly along the passage. Two closed doors are illuminated.

Will you try the door in the east wall? Turn to **138**. Or the door in the west wall? Turn to **151**. Or will you advance further along the passage? Turn to **172**.

120

The corridor is broad and slopes steadily downward towards a yellow light! Could you have found Ausbach at last? Covering the lantern, you tiptoe down the corridor. Turn to **313**.

121

As you hesitate, the creature springs at you.

'Now you will perish!' it screams. Roll against the creature's Dexterity (8). If it succeeds, turn to **259**.

If it fails, you aim your pistol and fire. You may fire one, two or three bullets as you wish, remembering to roll against your Dexterity for accuracy. Total the damage you have caused and deduct the number of bullets fired from your Character Profile. Whatever happens, turn to **339**.

122

You just manage to catch your breath before the smoke engulfs you. Even so, as you grope towards the door, your eyes and skin begin to smart. The door handle turns and you tumble from the cabin, slamming the door behind you. For a moment you rest on hands and knees, panting for breath, but the sound of other passengers approaching spurs you to rise. Like a drunk, you reel back along the corridor, locate your own cabin and collapse upon the bed. You have survived a poison gas trap but have lost 4 points of Stamina. Turn to **338**.

123

Your gunfire tears through the god, gouging deep into the plaster behind him. Immediately, the lights flicker out and you are plunged into darkness. Groping for your lantern,

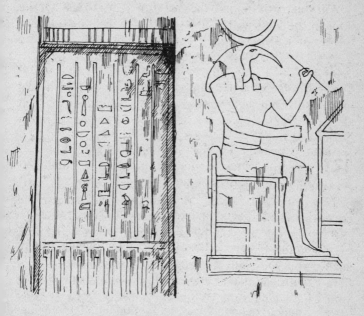

you uncover it. The picture, ruined by your gunfire, is still on the wall, but the god has disappeared. There is nothing left to do but to pass through the gilded door. Turn to **160**.

124

As you and Harold retreat towards the doorway, a gang of bogies rush towards you. Roll four dice and note the total on your Character Profile. This figure is the total Stamina of the bogies and it must be reduced to zero if you are to slay them all.

You swing the sword and it scythes into the creatures, lopping off arms, heads and legs. Roll against your Strength. If you succeed, you inflict the roll of two six-sided dice-worth of damage on the bogies. If you fail, you will only inflict one die roll's worth of damage. If the bogies' Stamina is reduced to zero, turn to **83**.

If the bogies survive your attack, they swarm around you. Roll against their Dexterity of 9. If they succeed, their teeth and claws tear 3 points of Stamina from you. If this reduces your level to zero, turn to **63**.

Now return and repeat the second paragraph of this section. The battle will proceed in this fashion until either you or the bogies win.

125

Dashing forward, you hurl yourself at Ausbach. As you leap, he senses your movement and spins around! Roll against your Dexterity. If you succeed, turn to **260**. If you fail, turn to **360**.

126

You pull the ashen wand from your jacket, while Ausbach continues his vile incantation. Can such a puny stick defeat a mad magician? You hook your arm back and cast the warrior's gift up into the air. The wind ceases and once again you hear the ponderous hum of the airship's engines. Ausbach is clearly perturbed by the storm's sudden end. He stands slack-shouldered and the inhuman light dies in his eyes.

'What sorcery can quell the wind lord's passion?' he cries. 'What magic have you squandered to aid you, meddling fool?'

As if in answer, the clouds ahead of the airship burst

apart and the wild hunt pours into view.

'We ride! We ride!' comes the cry of the dead warrior's retinue. Bony corpse-hounds surge towards Ausbach. Gnarled dead hands hold hunting spears at the ready.

'So!' jeers Ausbach. 'You would summon the hunters of souls against me? How can they seize me when I have no soul to give?'

The riders' leader turns his dead eyes upon you. 'It is true, we cannot tear him from this world. Yet a soul is the price we exact for our aid. You have called us here. You must pay the price!'

The warrior turns to his retinue and cries, 'We ride!' The riders take up their master's shout. The hounds snap at your heels and a spear pierces your chest.

'Join us,' cries one of the huntsmen, as the cold of death seeps through your body. The adventure is at an end for you.

127

Taking a firm grip on your chosen weapon, you stealthily advance upon the man, who appears engrossed in some bizarre ritual. He mumbles in a strange and unknown language. It is ugly, cruel and rasping. Raising your weapon, you are about to confront the thief when your foot squeaks on the polished wooden floor. The man's back stiffens, then he makes towards the sarcophagus. You have been detected. Turn to **310**.

128

The passage rises steadily and then opens out into the Grand Gallery. The walls are brightly painted with scenes from Khefu's life and great columns soar into the darkness overhead. Dwarfed by the scale of this gallery, you trudge up its central avenue, whilst your shadow stalks across the walls behind you. At the end of the Gallery, a huge statue rises from the floor into the shadows above. One of its

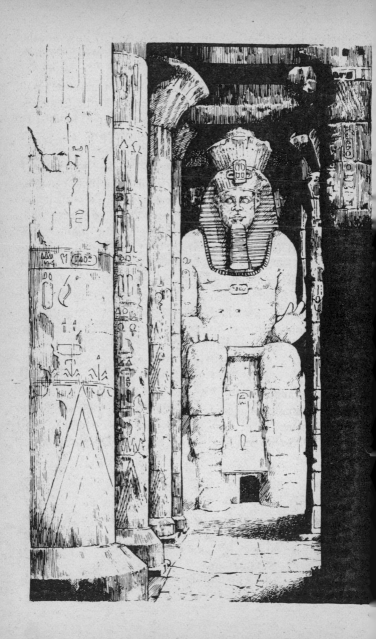

hands is turned up and outwards in warning. Between the statue's feet is a low archway that leads to the King's Chamber.

Will you proceed through the archway? Turn to **81**. Will you pause to examine the pictures which adorn the statue's legs? Turn to **67**. Or will you retrace your footsteps, to explore the Way of the Dead? Turn to **146**.

129

Opening the door, the light from your torch flickers across a large bedroom. A four-poster bed, draped with heavy velvet curtains, stands against the middle of the north wall. Opposite is a large fireplace and over the mantelpiece hangs a dark oil painting of a brooding seventeenth-century gentleman. There are two windows and, near the one set into the east wall, is a mahogany writing bureau.

Will you open the bureau? Turn to **104**. Draw back the curtains on the bed? Turn to **80**. Leave the room, either to try the double doors on the landing? Turn to **325**. Or to explore the north hallway? Turn to **245**.

130

You are standing in what must have been Khefu's treasure house. Ornate casks, gems, jewellery, gold plates and cups lie strewn across the floor, but pride of place seems to have been given to a strange, scythe-shaped, khephera sword

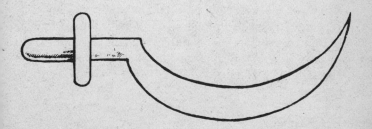

and a bizarre cap made out of crocodile skin. These lie upon a dais, before the bust of an ancient Egyptian. Khefu, perhaps?

Will you examine either the crocodile cap? Turn to **41**. Or the khephera sword? Turn to **17**. Or will you ignore these objects and pass out of the chamber down a corridor in the far wall? Turn to **30**.

131

You awake to find a police constable bending over you. His helmet is thrust back at a comic angle and he is scratching the side of his head with a pencil.

'I am afraid you are under arrest, sir,' he says. 'You seem to have been rather busy here tonight.'

You sigh. After all, who will believe your story? Your adventure is at an end.

132

You can suffer the blows of the dog's-head mace no more. Your skull cracks and you crash into oblivion. The dog man crouches over your prone form and howls in victory. Then he drags you away to his lair. This adventure is over for you.

133

The weapon slowly sinks through the membrane and you feel sure that you must be probing beyond the physical base of the sarcophagus. Suddenly the membrane puckers and gives way. Your arm plunges out of sight into a freezing cold and empty space! A fierce tingling sensation racks your arm like severe pins and needles. Roll against your Mentality. If you succeed, turn to **154**. If you fail, turn to **178**.

134

With a despairing cry, you lose your grip and fall away towards the forest below. The dark trees receive your broken body and hold you in their branches as a feast for carrion crows. The feasting done, your bones clatter into the forest's silent gloom.

135

The wheezing creaking corpse-thing seems intent upon ensnaring you. It probes the air in front with clumsy sweeps of its scrawny bandaged arms. You take a step backwards and your feet crunch on broken glass. The mummy halts, cocks its head as if listening, then turns to face you.

Boldly, you stand your ground then dodge the corpse-creature's first, ill-timed, attempt to ensnare you. Nimbly, you step to one side and raise your knobkerrie. Can you crush the thing's head with a single well-aimed blow? Roll against your Dexterity. If you succeed, turn to **57**.

If you fail, the mummy will attempt to ensnare you. Roll against the corpse-thing's Dexterity (6). If it succeeds, turn to **280**. If it fails, will you fight on? Turn to **74**. Or will you attempt to dodge past the mummy and flee the museum. Turn to **48**.

136

You are shaken awake by a bluff German policeman. He shouts at you in German and, when you mumble back in English, he grabs you by the shoulder and begins to drag you from the cockpit.

'You have much explaining to do,' he says, in a heavy accent. You groan. After all, who will believe your story in this sceptical scientific age? Your adventure ends here, in the hands of the German police.

137

You have lost 2 points of Endurance. The terrible chant of the faces goes on and on. A numbness creeps into your bones and you know the heads are chanting your very soul out of your body. Vile images fill your mind. You see Ausbach and his minions casting people within the circle. Your breath comes in short agonised bursts and you know you must act or risk death in the well of souls.

Match your Mentality against the soul tree's Mentality (7). If you succeed, turn to **159**. If you fail, turn to **93**.

138

When you enter this room, your torch beam plays across a mass of furniture covered in white dust sheets. As you pick your way among the humped shapes towards another door in the north wall, you notice one large chair is conspicuously free of the spectral covers. Lying on the seat is an eight-day-old newspaper. The front displays the headline: 'Unexplained disaster in Wales' and one paragraph has been savagely ringed in black ink. The very paragraph which mentions your involvement in these strange events and your home address!*

Will you now open the door in the north wall? Turn to **333**. Or will you return to the corridor? There you could open the door in the west wall, turn to **151**. Or you could go north along the corridor, turn to **172**.

139

As you delicately manoeuvre the key about the lock, trying to trip each barrel, you hear a curious dull click. A secret panel, next to the lock, springs back and a brass faucet squirts a jet of purple smoke into your face! Instantly, you abandon the skeleton key (strike it from your Character

---

* See 'Where the Shadows Stalk'.

Profile) and contrive to fall backwards out of the billowing smoke. Roll against your Dexterity. If you succeed, turn to **122**. If you fail, turn to **109**.

140

Whilst Ausbach is still unaware of your presence, you channel your thoughts through the cap and hurl a mental bolt at the back of his head. To overcome the Baron, you must match your Mentality against his Mentality (9) on the Conflict Table. If you succeed, turn to **214**. If you fail, turn to **272**.

141

Taking the infernal whistle from your mouth, you cry out, 'I command you to destroy my enemy!' As if in answer, there comes a shuddering growling roar and the east

window bursts inwards. A gout of burning stifling air invades the room, scattering the furniture. The horror is torn asunder, the curtains about the bed ignite and your clothes burst into flames. Screaming, you run towards the window and plunge to your death. The adventure is at an end.

142

You struggle in the scorpion's grip, but to no avail. Its sting flexes and then darts forward. A terrible burning pain erupts in your chest and the creature drops you, turning away to scuttle off into the darkness. You have been injected with a creeping poison and, until you find a cure, you will lose 1 point of Stamina every time you turn to an odd-numbered section in this adventure. Note this on your Character Profile.

Shaking, you stagger to your feet and go in search of an exit from the cavern. You find a narrow cleft in the far wall. Scrambling up, you squeeze through. Turn to **130**.

143

Not quick enough! You aim a blow at the hunchback's ugly head, but he manages to parry the blow, then swings his cleaver down towards your shoulder! Roll against the hunchback's Dexterity (6). If he fails, turn to **107**. If he succeeds, you suffer 3 points of damage to your Stamina. If your Stamina is reduced to zero, turn to **3**. If you survive the blow, you must try to retaliate, turn to **247**.

144

You are too slow. The bolt blasts across your chest, hurling you backwards along the walkway. You have lost 3 points of Stamina. Your body is numb; your only sensation the insistent tug of the wind. Ausbach stands over you and a leer of triumph contorts his odious features.

'Now you shall be my slave and your life-force my toy!' Your mind slides into a thankful oblivion. Turn to **25**.

145

To use the skeleton key, match your Dexterity against the door lock's complexity (8) on the Conflict Table. If you succeed, turn to **296**. If you fail, turn to **171**.

146

The Way of the Dead leads deep beneath the pyramid. It terminates in an unfinished chamber, carved from the bedrock of the plateau. Only one wall has been limed and painted and, raising the lantern, you examine the painting. It shows Anubis, god of the dead, supported by the ibis-headed god, Thoth, judging the souls of men. Some of the souls are invited to enter a bright boat, but others are cast into darkness on the left of the picture.

If you have the dark lantern, turn to **103**. Otherwise, you must make a Mentality roll. If you fail, you can find nothing more of interest in this room. You must retrace your steps to the room of the hieroglyphs, to explore the passage that leads to the Grand Gallery. Turn to **128**. However, if you succeed, turn to **103**.

147

Your thrust is ill-aimed, the swordstick merely pierces the creature's wrappings. For a moment the corpse-thing sways uncertainly, then it jerks its arms towards you.

Match the mummy's Dexterity (6) against your Dexterity on the Conflict Table. If the creature succeeds, turn to **280**. If it fails, will you fight on? Turn to **26**. Or will you attempt to escape? Turn to **82**.

148

Pulling Harold along behind, you run to the wall and heave a rusty great sword from the display. Enter the sword on your Character Profile as Great Sword 2D6/–. When you attack with the sword, roll against your Dexterity. If you are successful, the sword inflicts damage on the bogies' Stamina equivalent to the roll of two dice (2D6). Turn to **124**.

149

'See,' the creature mocks, 'you cannot harm me. Now prepare to die, mortal!'

The assassin-bug crouches and prepares to spring at you. Roll against the creature's Dexterity (8). If it succeeds, turn to **259**.

If it fails, you dodge the creature's pounce and draw your pistol. You may fire one, two or three bullets as you wish, remembering to roll against your Dexterity for accuracy. Total the damage you have caused and deduct the number of bullets fired from your Character Profile. Whatever happens, turn to **339**.

150

Thoth puts down his quill and steps out of the picture, raising a hand in greeting.

'Do not be afraid, mortal,' he says in a fluting voice. 'I mean you no harm. The creature you seek has already passed into the underworld and soon he will summon Het from the Outer Darkness. I cannot interfere directly in these events, but I can help you indirectly.'

If you have been poisoned by the scorpion or infected by the Hand of Glory, turn to **187**. Otherwise, you may ask Thoth a question. Will you ask about the pyramidion? Turn to **213**. Or will you ask how Ausbach can be destroyed? Turn to **226**.

151

You have entered a room in which the darkness is almost tangible. Shining the torch about, you see that walls, curtains and decorations are uniformly black. There is no carpet, only bare floorboards and upon these is chalked a red circle. Within the circle stands a fantastic table. Three hideous brazen dragons writhe upwards to form a tripod. Their jaws gape wide to support a circular green marble top, upon which rests a bronze box.

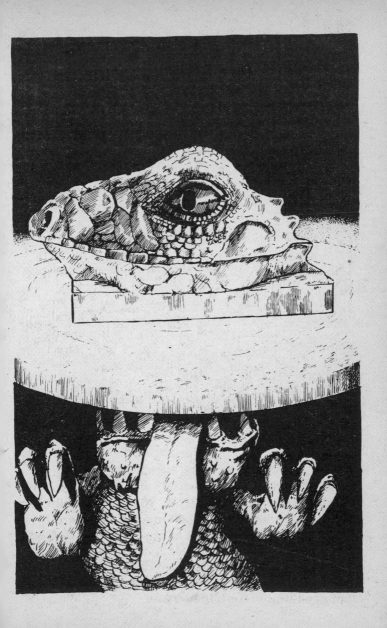

Will you examine the bronze box? Turn to **198**. Or will you return to the corridor? Here you could go north, turn to **172**. Or you could open the door in the east wall, turn to **138**.

152

Looking desperately about the room, you see that the painting above the mantelpiece is shimmering with a blood-red light. This must be the focus or gateway through which the succubus entered the room. Perhaps if you can destroy it, you can destroy the horror too? If you have bullets, will you blast the painting with your pistol? Turn to **174**. Or will you struggle across the room and tear the painting down? Turn to **194**.

153

Skilfully, you dodge the creature and run towards the tripod. It supports a flat shelf, upon which sits an earthenware jar with a dog's head for a lid. You grasp the object and pull off the lid. Inside is a clay replica of a human heart. Even as the dog man flings himself upon you, the heart is plummeting to the ground. The creature smashes into you and carries you on into the tripod.

You lie on your back as the dog man prepares to rip out your throat; yet, before he can act, a strange transformation takes place. Smoke begins to boil from the creature's chest. He rolls off you, clutching at the place where his heart should be. He slavers, chokes, then collapses – dead. You have lost 1 point of Stamina from the fall. You struggle to your feet and stride purposefully towards the Guardian. Turn to **77**.

154

With a gasp, you pull your arm free of the rubbery membrane. Your coat smoulders and gives off a rank musty odour. The skin of your hand is puckered, white and flaky –

like the skin of a corpse – and your weapon is stained with the mark of rust or rot. Whether your arm plunged into another dimension or through time, you are unsure but, whatever happened here, the experience has cost you 1 point of Endurance.

In the distance you can now make out the sound of shouting and an insistent alarm bell. It is time to leave the museum. Turn to **205**.

155

Delicately, you manoeuvre the skeleton key about the lock. Your intention is to trip each barrel and persuade the lock to yield. At last, you are rewarded by a satisfying dull click. You stand and prise apart the two halves of the trunk. A vile stench greets you, as a miasma of grey gaseous smoke wafts into the cabin. You gag, stagger backwards and lose 1 point of Stamina.

The smoke disperses to reveal the trunk's curious and repellent interior. Each half is filled with hard-packed, evil-smelling, black, cemetery earth. This forms a mould in the shape of a seated humanoid figure! Green scum oozes from the earth's surface and white things wriggle from the light of day. The trunk is a portable grave! Baron Ausbach is either a macabre eccentric or an unwholesome ghoul!

Your horrid musing is suddenly interrupted. A floorboard creaks, a wickedly curved dagger glints and a sineous arm clamps around your neck! Roll against your Dexterity. If you succeed, turn to **8**. If you fail, turn to **15**.

156

If you still have a weapon, you cunningly conceal it beneath your coat. Then you make your way home by a circuitous route, for the streets about the museum are now crowded with an assortment of police vehicles and running constables.

You can explain nothing of the night's events, but you are sure of one thing: it is time to team your daredevil skills with the knowledge and sage advice of your friend, the scholar and explorer, Charles Petrie-Smith. Turn to **175**.

157

A light plank door creaks open to reveal a neglected laboratory cum store-room. A study table is piled high with dusty glass jars, test tubes and piping. In one corner is a grinning human skeleton. Bookshelves line the rest of the walls, sagging under the weight of musty mildewed tomes. However, your attention is drawn to a pile of wooden crates, which exhibit no sign of age or grime. The top crate contains a most puzzling artefact: a gleaming brass lantern with a curious cone-shaped attachment welded to its front.

Will you examine this object more closely? Turn to **193**. Or will you continue with your descent of the spiral staircase? Turn to **211**.

158

With a shudder of horror, you step back. Lose 1 point of Endurance. The hand is shrunken and withered with age. Strange red symbols are tattooed on the back of each of its gnarled fingers. As you stare unbelievingly, it drops off the table and runs across the floor towards you!

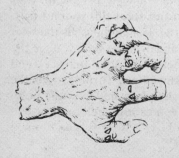

Will you turn and flee through the carved archway? Turn to **120**. Or will you try to crush this monstrosity underfoot? If this is your choice, roll against your Dexterity. If you succeed, turn to **217**. If you fail, turn to **240**.

159

With all your will, you tear your mind free of the hypnotic chant of the dead faces, then drag yourself and Harold around the edge of the pit to the entrance of another tunnel. Turn to **197**.

160

The door opens on a twilight world of grey rolling hills and dead vegetation. Oppressed by the landscape, you trudge wearily up the nearest hill. With each new step, the grass beneath your feet crumbles into dust. At last you crest the hill and look down upon a vast river, whose dark waters flow sluggishly through the barren land. The far bank is out of sight but, below and to your left, you see a crumbling wharf which juts out into the water. Moored to its side is an ancient ferry.

Descending to the wharf, you find it is made of bones that crunch beneath your feet. The boat at its side is both wormeaten and rotten. A dark figure, hidden in the folds of a black habit, rears up out of the stern of the boat. With a thin hand, he waves you on to the ferry.

The timbers of the ferry squelch and groan beneath your weight and the smell of mould and decay fills your nostrils. The ferryman lifts a pole off the deck and pushes the boat out into the silent waters. Gazing over the side, you see the dark water is filled with currents and eddies that suck and claw at the ferry, but without any effect. Turning to ask the ferryman about this, you see him hunched over the pole, his cloak flapping in a wind you cannot feel!

'The Styx is a river of time, mortal. You cross the dimensions from the edge of life to the realm of the dead.'

On the far bank, the ferry beaches on a mud-flat and the ferryman extends a skeletal hand for payment. If you have the gold coin, you may use it now, turn to **302**. Alternatively, you may present him with an artefact of your choice, turn to **329**. Or you can refuse to pay and leap from the ferry. Turn to **348**.

161

The corridor ends in a large window which overlooks the woods to the south of the house. There is a door in the west wall marked Bathroom and an unmarked door in the east wall. Will you try this door? Turn to **129**. Or will you return to the landing to try the double doors? Turn to **325**. Or explore the north hallway? Turn to **245**.

162

At last you pick out the correct frequency and hail Munich. You tell them the mailplane has developed engine trouble, and you wish to land in order to transfer the mail to the airship *Lucretia*. The air traffic controller replies that the airship has yet to arrive and you are cleared to land. Turn to **89**.

163

There is nothing of interest in the pockets of the hunchback's coat. The body's only mark of identification is emblazoned upon the back of the cold right hand: a gaudy tattoo of a serpent devouring its own tail beneath the legend 'Apep'. You move away from the body, yet something draws you back.

The hunchback has only just expired, yet his hand was cold and chill – as if he had been dead for a long time! You kneel by the body and touch the neck. It is cold and the veins seem knotted, as if filled with clotted blood. On an impulse you pull back the musty mud-stained shirt and reveal a yawning chasm beneath. The creature had no heart! Roll against your Mentality. If you fail, lose 1 point of Endurance.

Now it is time to explore the rest of the house. Steeling your resolve, you leave the kitchen via a door in the east wall. Turn to **34**.

164

With a sharp crack the bolt bursts and you rush into the

cabin. A macabre sight greets your eyes. The pilot lies face up, half in and half out of his seat. His neck has been torn open and a Luger pistol is gripped in the dead fingers of his right hand. Did he kill himself?

Your answer comes in the form of a long and malevolent hiss. Out of the corner of your eye, you catch sight of a pair of giant spider-like legs, scrabbling for a hold on the co-pilot's seat. The hair on the nape of your neck begins to rise and a cold sweat breaks out upon your forehead. Turn to **86**.

165

Match your Dexterity against the lock's complexity (8) on the Conflict Table. If you succeed, turn to **155**. If you fail, turn to **139**.

Plunging your hand in the jar, you squeeze the brain and hear Ausbach cry out in agony. Instantly, the flaming hand disappears and you turn to see the Baron feebly clutching the altar. You squeeze again, and he clutches his head, swaying from side to side, then crumples to the ground. Where the brain was, dust now fills your hand; where the Baron died, there are only his clothes and a brownish dust.

Then a hissing draws your eyes back to the pillar of fire. Emerging from a nebulous haze at the centre of the fire is a monstrous snake head! You must act swiftly to close the gateway Ausbach has created. Your only hope is to destroy the pyramidion. But how?

Will you use Thoth's mace? Turn to **342**. The khephera sword, knobkerrie or swordstick? Turn to **355**. The dragon whistle? Turn to **319**. Or will you snatch the pyramidion from the altar and hurl it into the pit? Turn to **224**.

167

Shocked, you lose 1 point of Endurance. If this reduces your level to zero, turn to **228**. The creature lurches into the air and, with a screech, flies at you!

It will attack you with its vicious talons and curved beak. There is no chance to run away, so how will you defend yourself? With the khephera sword? Turn to **249**. With the crocodile cap? Turn to **303**. With Thoth's mace, the knobkerrie or the swordstick? Turn to **326**. Or with the pistol? Turn to **347**.

168

Instantly, you interpose the scarab between your body and the bolt. At the last moment, before the electricity bursts upon you, it arcs upwards into the scarab. The ancient talisman glows incandescent blue and you lose 1 point of Stamina. Then, with a loud crack, it discharges the bolt back towards its maker. The plasma explodes across Ausbach's chest and he crashes backwards over the rail.

With a great effort he struggles to his feet, climbs upon the handrail, perches for an instant, then leaps towards you. Instead of crashing at your feet in a wind-blown heap, his whole body seems to split apart, transforming into a monstrous flapping beast. Powerful talons grip your

shoulders and leathern wings bear you up and away from the *Lucretia*. The beast's wild eyes bore into your own and the vile familiar voice taunts you.

'You shall be my slave and your life-force my toy!' Your mind slides into a thankful oblivion. Turn to **25**.

169

Desperately, you and Harold try to close the door in the face of the slavering bogie horde, but one creature, half-man, half-pig, jams itself in the doorway. You must beat it off.

You step forward and strike the creature. Roll against your Dexterity. If you succeed, you inflict 2 points of damage to the creature's Stamina (7). If the bogie is slain, turn to **225**.

If the bogie still lives, it retaliates. Roll against the creature's Dexterity. If it succeeds, you lose 2 points from your Stamina. If you are reduced to zero, turn to **63**.

Now match your Strength against the creature's Strength (6) on the Conflict Table. If you succeed, you thrust the creature back into the arms of its fellows, turn to **225**. If you fail, you must fight on – return and repeat the second paragraph of this section.

170

You direct the jet over the beast. Its vile taunts are silenced and it cringes. Then, with startling speed, the assassin-bug runs towards you, thrusts its soft body past you and scuttles away into the plane's fuselage. An instant later the side door bursts open and an icy wind rips through the plane.

Now you must try to fly the aircraft. If you fired five or more bullets during the battle, turn to **287**. If you fired less, or beat the creature with the fire extinguisher alone, turn to **372**.

171

As you crouch to tinker with the lock, the door handle twists and the door opens. The skeleton key is wrenched from your hand and you topple over on to your back. (Delete the key from your Character Profile.) A large man in an ill-fitting blue suit towers over you. He wears a pair of dark glasses and points a short-barrelled pistol at your chest.

'I just pressed the steward's bell,' he rasps in a thick American accent. 'Beat it!'

Obviously, this is not the thief from the British Museum. You stammer some feeble excuse, scramble to your feet and hurry away along the corridor. When you have recovered from this embarrassing blunder, will you visit the mysterious Baron's cabin? Turn to **192**. Or will you abandon the investigation and return to your cabin? Turn to **45**.

172

As you creep along the corridor, you discover two more closed doors. The one in the west wall is locked and defeats your best efforts with the skeleton key. Will you instead turn to the door in the east wall? Turn to **333**. Or will you continue along the corridor? Turn to **50**.

173

You are gripped in the creature's powerful claws and drawn towards its sting. Roll against the creature's Dexterity (8). If it succeeds, turn to **142**.

If the scorpion fails, you struggle to escape. Match your Strength against the creature's Strength (6) on the Conflict

Table. If you fail, return and repeat this section. If you succeed, you break free and may attack the scorpion. Will you fire your gun? Turn to **264**. Use the knobkerrie or swordstick? Turn to **231**. Or will you pipe upon the dragon whistle? Turn to **200**.

174

Pulling the pistol from your coat, you empty the entire magazine into the painting. (Delete all the remaining bullets from your Character Profile.) The bullets rip into the painting, tearing it to shreds. Instantly, the succubus begins to shrivel, to collapse in upon itself, until all that remains is a foetid pool of water on the carpet. Shaking, you stumble from the room. Later, will you open the double doors on the landing? Turn to **325**. Or explore the north hallway? Turn to **245**.

175

You awake in the morning having recovered half of any Stamina and Endurance lost during last night's struggles. (If your Strength was impaired, that returns to its original value.)

After breakfast, you hurry out to the post office and send an urgent telegram to Petrie-Smith: 'Need your help. Strange work ahead. Come quickly.' Then you return home and examine the morning newspapers.

Most editions carry news of last night's escapade: 'Desecration of British Museum!' yells one headline. 'Trail of Destruction' shouts another. You pass the afternoon reading their lurid accounts. Petrie-Smith arrives late in the evening and together you discuss events so far.

If you battled with the corpse-man thief, turn to **196**. If you fought the mummy, turn to **218**.

176

As the maidservant cunningly circles, preparing for a new attack, you rush at her. With one hand you grab her wrist, with the other you try to prise her fingers from the dagger's hilt. The woman struggles furiously. Match your Strength against the maidservant's Strength (8) on the Conflict Table. If you succeed, turn to **191**.

If you fail, the maidservant struggles free and slashes at you with the dagger. Roll against her Dexterity (9). If she succeeds, the blade slashes 2 points from your Stamina. If you are reduced to zero, turn to **250**. If not, you desperately try to trap the woman's dagger arm. Return to the beginning of this section.

177

Can you evade the dog man's murderous clutches and flee from the temple? Match your Dexterity against the dog man's Dexterity (8) on the Conflict Table. If you succeed, you escape. Turn to **337**.

If you fail, the creature aims a blow at you. Roll against the creature's Dexterity. If it succeeds, you have 2 points smashed from your Stamina. If you are reduced to zero, turn to **132**.

If you still live, you may try to complete your escape by repeating the first paragraph of this section. Otherwise, you could battle on with the khephera sword, Thoth's mace, the knobkerrie or the swordstick. Turn to **237**. Or you could blast it with your pistol. Turn to **202**.

You awake on the floor, half in and half out of the display case. Your head throbs from the fall and your arm feels numb. Staggering to your feet, you notice that your coat smoulders and gives off a rank musty odour. The skin of your hand is puckered, white and flaky – like the skin of a corpse. Your weapon is nowhere to be seen. (Strike it from your Character Profile.) This experience has cost you 2 points of Endurance.

Now you can hear the sound of clattering feet and agitated shouts reverberating through the museum. The authorities have been aroused! It is time to flee the Egyptian room. Turn to **205**.

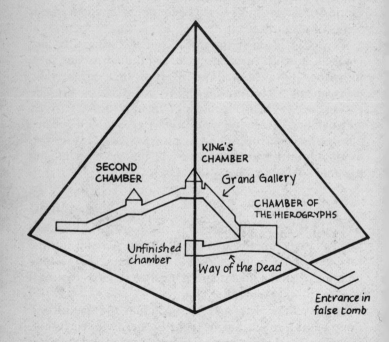

SECOND CHAMBER

KING'S CHAMBER

Grand Gallery

CHAMBER OF THE HIEROGRYPHS

Unfinished chamber

Way of the Dead

Entrance in false tomb

The entrance is hidden behind an imposing façade near the east face of the pyramid. Together, you pass between the ancient columns and trek through countless rooms until you reach a crude chamber. Here, the torn body of an Arab lies on the floor and a broad flight of steps descends into the earth. Lighting the lantern, you begin your descent and Petrie-Smith watches after you until you disappear from sight.

As you go deeper, the air becomes colder. You find yourself in a wide passage, lined with plain stone slabs. Your footsteps echo hollowly as you march between the walls, and the lantern's light flickers in the cold gloom. The passage ends in a large chamber, whose walls are covered with paintings and hieroglyphs. You are faced with a choice of ways. Will you fork left on to the Way of the Dead? Turn to **146**. Or turn right into the passage that leads up into the pyramid's Grand Gallery? Turn to **128**.

You are faced by another gang of bogies, who hiss and jabber as they rush towards you. Roll four dice and note the total on your Character Profile. This figure is the total Stamina of all the bogies and it must be reduced to zero if you are to kill them all.

You level the pistol and fire. You may fire one, two or three bullets, rolling against your Dexterity for each shot. If you hit, total the damage you have caused and deduct it from the bogies' Stamina. If they are all killed, turn to **225**.

However, if you miss or if they survive, they swarm around you. Roll against their Dexterity of 9. If they succeed, their teeth and claws rip 3 points from your Stamina. If this reduces your rating to zero, turn to **63**. Otherwise, you may now try to escape through the archway door. Turn to **268**.

181

The radio is located in the bulkhead above you. Slipping a voice mask over your head, you switch on. Now, can you locate the right frequency to hail the Munich aerodrome? Match your Mentality against the radio's controls (8) on the Conflict Table. If you succeed, turn to **162**. If you fail, you will have to attempt an unauthorised landing. Turn to **89**.

182

The trunk is massive: a man-sized construction of oak boards, bound with iron braces. It looks very old. The wood is stained black and marked with deep scuffs and scars. A strange musty smell, as of damp earth or rotting leaves, seems to cling about the thing. Finally, you note the sole mark of ownership: a battered brass nameplate, stained with verdigris. You can just follow the corroded letters of a name, done in a heavy gothic script: Baron von Ausbach. The trunk is locked; you will need the skeleton key to open it. Turn to **165**. Otherwise, you can examine the object on the table. Turn to **84**.

183

As you wait, body braced against the handrail, you catch snatches of Ausbach's vile incantation to Wendigo, Lord of the Winds. His actions excite the shroud of electricity about his body; it shimmers in bands of blue and red. Finally, Ausbach emits a blood-curdling shriek, which rises even above the storm's fury, and throws his arms out towards you. A dazzling coil of electricity leaps at you. Roll against your Dexterity. If you fail, turn to **168**. If you succeed, turn to **144**.

184

Your shambling opponent lets out a final despairing groan, staggers backwards, then crashes to the floor. Appalled by the violence of this encounter, you collapse into a chair to recover. Will you search the corpse? Turn to **163**. Or will you leave the kitchen, via a door in the east wall, to explore the rest of the mansion? Turn to **34**.

185

The door opens to reveal a devastated room. The mattress has slipped from the bed. The drawers of a tallboy have been rifled and their contents scattered across the floor. Mystified, you turn to leave and your foot clips a small metal box. You pick the object up and, in the torchlight, see that you have retrieved a silver cigarette case. It is engraved with the name Harold Lathers. Baffled by this discovery, you close the door.

Will you continue along the south hall? Turn to **161**. Return to the landing and open the double doors? Turn to **325**. Or explore the north hall? Turn to **245**.

186

While you ponder whether to blast your way through the door with your pistol, the plane seems to slide into a nose dive. As the engines begin to whine, you are thrown off balance against the cabin door. The bolt bursts and you are thrown forward on to the pilot's corpse! Roll against your Mentality. If you succeed, turn to **39**. If you fail, turn to **102**.

187

Thoth passes his hands over your head and a feeling of well-being fills your body. You have been cured (delete your ills from the Character Profile) and you have also regained 2 points of Stamina.

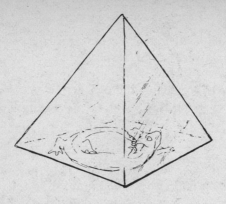

If you want to learn about the pyramidion, turn to **213**. If you do not, and you have the khephera sword, turn to **248**. Otherwise, turn to **270**.

188

Shocked by this travesty of nature, you lose 2 points of Endurance. If this reduces you to zero, turn to **254**. The hand is shrunken and withered with age. Strange red symbols are tattooed on the back of each of its gnarled fingers. As you watch, it leaps on to your chest! Jumping back, you feel it clamber up your body and clasp your throat. Roll against the hand's Strength (8). If it succeeds, it crushes 2 points of Stamina from your body. If this reduces you to zero, turn to **254**. However if it fails, you can try to tear it off. Match your Strength against the hand's Strength on the Conflict Table. If you succeed, turn to **273**. If you fail, turn to **300**.

189

Shocked by the ka's appearance, you lose 2 points of Endurance. If this reduces your level to zero, turn to **228**. You stagger back as, with a screech, it leaps into the air and hurls itself upon you!

The ka's talons rake through the air towards you. Roll against the ka's Dexterity of 8. If it succeeds, its talons rip across your body, tearing 2 points of Stamina from you. If your Stamina is reduced to zero, turn to **228**.

If you survive, you must select a weapon, as there is no possibility of running away. Will you choose the khephera sword? Turn to **249**. The crocodile cap? Turn to **303**. Thoth's mace, the knobkerrie or the swordstick? Turn to **326**. Or the pistol? Turn to **347**.

190

The weapon slowly sinks through the membrane until you feel certain that you must be probing beyond the physical base of the sarcophagus. Then the membrane's surface shimmers and you find yourself staring at the ancient wooden base of the sarcophagus. Your weapon is now embedded in the planking, with part of it thrust right through the base. You tug with all your might but to no avail.

Now you can hear the sound of clattering feet and agitated shouts reverberating through the museum. The authorities have been aroused! It is time to flee the Egyptian room. Turn to **205**.

191

Savagely, you tear the maidservant's gloved fingers from about the dagger's hilt. The weapon clatters to the floor. You follow up this success with a rough shoulder barge, which sends the woman reeling back against the wall. As she struggles to her feet, you stoop and grab the dagger. Now it seems the advantage is with you. Will you attack the defenceless maidservant or leave the cabin?

Before you can decide, the maidservant performs an astonishing transformation. Accompanied by a weird, inhuman, hissing sound she tears away a waxen face mask to reveal the cold repellent features of a serpent man! Roll against your Mentality. If you succeed, turn to **208**. If you fail, turn to **252**.

192

You hurry to cabin 3 and boldly knock upon the door. There is no reply from within, but you are startled by a voice from behind.

'I am afraid the Baron and his nurse aren't in their cabin.' You turn to face a steward, who continues, 'They went aft to check their luggage.'

As the steward walks away, you surreptitiously try the door handle. The door is locked. Will you pick the lock with the skeleton key, if you have it? Turn to **206**. Or will you try to force the door? Turn to **255**.

You pick up the lamp and are surprised to find it still contains fuel. The mechanism seems most eccentric. Instead of a wick surrounded by a glass cylinder, this lamp has a prism which appears to direct light in one direction only: through the brass cone welded to the lamp's side.

Searching your pockets, you discover some matches and light this curious artefact. You are startled by the lamp's peculiar property: it casts a beam of darkness. Where the beam falls, solid objects appear to dissolve into nothing. Will you take the dark lantern? If this is your choice, enter the artefact on your Character Profile. You leave the room and continue to descend the spiral staircase. Turn to **211**.

As you struggle across the room, bearing the succubus-horror with you, the thing sucks 3 more points of Stamina from your body. If you are reduced to zero, turn to **212**. If not, read on.

With both hands you tear the painting from the wall and smash its frame upon the fireplace. Instantly, the horror begins to shrivel, to collapse in upon itself, until all that remains is a foetid pool of water on the carpet. Shaking, you stumble from the room. Later, will you open the double doors on the landing? Turn to **325**. Or explore the north hallway? Turn to **245**.

The creature visibly wilts under the cold stream of gas. It splutters and gurgles, then its legs collapse and it topples off the dead pilot. You finish the assassin-bug with crushing blows from the empty extinguisher's cylinder, then push the mangled body aft into the aircraft's fuselage.

Now you must try to fly the plane. If you fired five or more bullets during the battle, turn to **323**. If you fired less,

or beat the creature with the fire extinguisher alone, turn to
372. ✦

196

Petrie-Smith listens carefully to your account, then sits
back in his armchair and gazes thoughtfully into the fire.

After a few minutes' meditation he turns to you and says,
'In Egyptian legend there are tales of sorcerers who
travelled great distances in an instant, by means of magic
"Thaati" gateways. They called it "flying on the wings of
Horus". It sounds to me as if the thief, or his master,
constructed such a gateway in the British Museum.
However, he or they would require another, identical,
gateway at the home base. I know of a sarcophagus which is
the exact twin of the one you describe; it is part of the
collection of the Egyptologist, Sir Roderick Lathers, at
Shandwick House in Kent.

'However, your description of the thief and the symbol
of the serpent devouring its tail disturbs me. In Egyptian

mythology that symbol belongs to Het the Destroyer, a
fiendish deity who consumed those souls of the dead, who
were found wanting in the judgement of Anubis. Some of
these spirits she returned to earth as her servitors, hence
legends of the undead. Could it be that the thief is indeed a
corpse-man?

'We must tread carefully, for once again I fear dark forces are at work. Tomorrow I shall follow up my assertions in the British Museum Library, while you collect the tools needed for a trip to Shandwick House!' Turn to **236**.

197

'At the end of the tunnel is the means of our escape,' declares Harold. 'When Ausbach kidnapped me from Shandwick House, he brought me here through some kind of dimensional gateway. Follow me.' Together, you plunge down the tunnel and out into a hexagonal-shaped room. The centre of the floor is a smoking black abyss.

'See,' says Harold. 'This is the dimensional gateway. We need only leap into the centre to return to England.'

Without hesitating, Harold Lathers leaps into the darkness and disappears from view! For a moment you stare in disbelief, then spurred by the sound of unnatural baying and slavering from behind, you leap too! Turn to **215**.

198

Boldly, you step within the red chalk circle and advance to the Dragon Table. The bronze box is fashioned in the shape of a serpent's head, but it only contains a sickly-smelling incense. It is the turn of the green marble table top to arouse your curiosity. Under the torchlight it seems to glow with a strange, almost pulsing, green luminescence – an effect compounded by a disquieting spiral pattern which seems to lead the eye down into the table top. Roll against your Mentality. If you succeed, turn to **232**. If you fail, turn to **216**.

199

Clutching the jar, you rush forward, shouting Ausbach's name over the roar of the flames. The Baron turns and his obscene laughter fills the air. He raises a hand and points towards the pillar of fire.

'Fool! You are too late! Your meddling is over. I have opened the gateway to Het!' His hand drops and his voice dies as he sees what you clutch in your hand.

You dip your hand in the jar but already Ausbach is passing his hands frantically through the air and his spell begins to grip your mind. Pit your Mentality against Ausbach's Mentality (9) on the Conflict Table. If you succeed, turn to **301**. If you fail, turn to **322**.

200

As you blow upon the whistle, you lose 1 point of Endurance. Your piping is strangely silent, but the effect upon the creature is quite startling. Its movements slow down and it seems to shudder. Then its body begins to crack, several legs collapse and the creature lurches to the right. Its vicious serrated claws open and shut feebly, then topple from its body to smash upon the cavern floor. A myriad cracks run across the scorpion's brittle body and it crumbles into harmless pottery shards. Above, something large flaps away into the darkness.

You turn away into the cavern and search for an exit. Finding a narrow cleft in the cavern wall, you scramble up and squeeze through the gap. Turn to **130**.

'I should say,' observes Petrie-Smith, 'that Ausbach provided us with this sport to cover his entry into the pyramid.' The veteran investigator is proved right when, a few minutes later, Harold Lathers breathlessly appears.

'The guard at the pyramid has disappeared!' he cries.

'Come,' says Petrie-Smith, 'we have no time to lose.' He hurries you back to the camp fire, then disappears into his tent. He emerges a few moments later and thrusts a canvas package into your hand.

'Here is a lantern, so much more dependable than those new-fangled electric contraptions, and some food. Now off you go! Retrieve your pyramidion and seal Ausbach in the underworld. I am sure you will only be away for a couple of hours.'

Add the following to your Character Profile under Possessions: Lantern, 3 points of food and a water canteen. Each time you eat some of the food you will recover 1 or more points of Stamina to a maximum of 3 points.

As you walk towards the pyramid, you reload your pistol. Turn to **179**.

202

You draw your pistol and squeeze the trigger. You may fire one, two or three bullets at the frenzied dog man. Remember to roll against your Dexterity each time you fire, for accuracy. Total the damage you have caused and strike the number of bullets fired from your Character Profile. If the dog man is slain, turn to **23**.

If the creature still lives, he will continue the struggle. Roll against the dog man's Dexterity (8). If he succeeds, his mace will smash 2 points from your Stamina. If you are reduced to zero, turn to **132**.

If you survive, you could continue the combat by repeating the first paragraph of this section. Otherwise, you could make use of the khephera sword, Thoth's mace, the knobkerrie or the swordstick. Turn to **237**. Or you could try to escape. Turn to **177**.

203

Frantically, you press your ear to the door but can hear nothing. It is time to apply your shoulder to the task of bursting open the door. Match your Strength against the bolt's Strength (5) on the Conflict Table. If you succeed, turn to **164**. If you fail, turn to **186**.

204

Moving along the corridor, you come across a door set in the east wall. Will you try this door? Turn to **185**. Will you carry on along the corridor? Turn to **161**. Or will you return to the landing where you can either open the double doors? Turn to **325**. Or explore the north hallway? Turn to **245**.

Swiftly you make your way back through the museum, aware that the formerly deserted galleries now hum with activity. The museum authorities have been roused by your intrusion.

At the head of the marble staircase, in the Chinese room, the sound of hobnails obliges you to dodge behind a display case. Moments later a police constable and a security man emerge into the gallery and hurry away towards the Egyptian room. Once they are gone, you slip from your hiding place and descend to the street. Turn to **156**.

206

To use the skeleton key, match your Dexterity against the door lock's complexity (9) on the Conflict Table. If you succeed, you gain entry to the cabin. Turn to **220**. If you fail, turn to **235**.

207

You are faced by another gang of bogies, who hiss and jabber as they run towards you. Roll four dice and note the total on your Character Profile. This figure represents the total Stamina of all the bogies in the gang and it must be reduced to zero if you are to kill them all.

Plucking out a corpse dust pot you fling it at the creatures. (Strike a pot from your Character Profile.) Roll against your Dexterity. If you succeed, the pot bursts among them, inflicting damage equal to the roll of three dice. If the bogies' Stamina is reduced to zero, turn to **106**.

If the bogies survive, or, if you missed, they press home their attack. Roll against their Dexterity of 9. If they succeed, their teeth and claws tear 3 points of Stamina from your body. If this reduces your Stamina to zero, turn to **63**. If not, you can try escaping through the archway door. Turn to **268**.

208

This incredible transformation has cost you 1 point of Endurance. Nevertheless, you steel your nerves, for now you hold the creature's weapon. Or do you? The serpent man's face is utterly alien and unfathomable, yet you sense by the creature's stance and stealthy movement that he is cunning. With careful deliberation, the creature peels the maidservant's gloves from its hands to reveal sharp talons. Its cold serpent eyes never once stop staring into your own.

Before the serpent man can strike, you attack. Roll against your Dexterity. If you succeed, the dagger slashes 2 points from the creature's Stamina. If your attack has slain the creature, turn to **279**. If it still lives, read on.

Now the serpent man attacks, slashing at you with his talons. Roll against his Dexterity (9). If he succeeds, you suffer a wound of 2 points from your Stamina. If you are reduced to zero, turn to **233**. If not, strike back by repeating the second paragraph of this section. You continue to trade blows with your reptilian adversary, until either you or he is slain.

Your ramshackle opponent yelps with fury, thrusts you away and then swings the meat cleaver at you. Roll against his Dexterity (6). If he succeeds, the cleaver crushes 3 points from your Stamina.

Now it is your turn to react. Will you charge the hunchback in an effort to disarm him? Turn to **312**. Or will you continue to trade deadly blows with the candleholder? If this is your choice, roll against your Dexterity. If you succeed, the candleholder wounds the hunchback, causing 2 points of damage to his Stamina (15). Whether you are successful or not, the hunchback will counter-attack. Return and repeat the first paragraph.

The battle proceeds in this way until either you or the hunchback succumb to your wounds. If you are defeated, turn to **3**. If the hunchback is slain, turn to **184**.

210

If you have reduced the creature's Stamina to zero, turn to **230**.

If not, the creature taunts, 'See you cannot slay me. Now prepare to die!'

The assassin-bug crouches and prepares to spring at you. It has a Dexterity of 8. If it succeeds, turn to **259**. If it fails, and you still have bullets, turn to **314**. If your magazine is empty, turn to **352**.

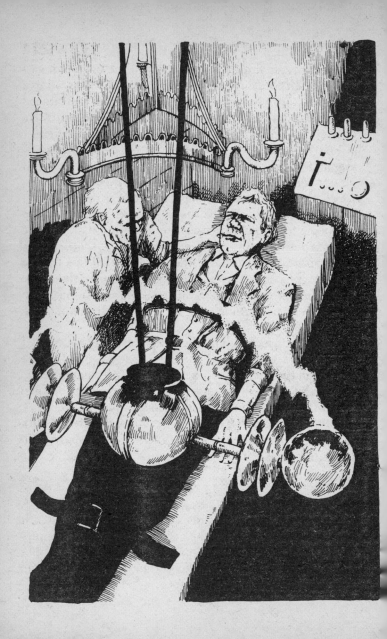

The spiral stairway leads you at last to the edge of a vast hall. You emerge on to a wooden balcony. To your left, is a stone staircase which descends into a great hall. Tall arched windows illuminate decayed tapestries and an impressive display of weaponry: swords, spears, daggers and shields.

Yet this faded medieval splendour has been invaded by the rude trappings of the twentieth century. The warm breeze you felt on the stairs is supplied by a copper retort, which bubbles and steams at the top of a pile of pipes, storage cylinders and valves. There is also the deep throbbing hum of electricity; generators and batteries line an entire wall, while static electricity rises spectacularly along spiral conductors. In the middle of all this bizarre machinery, like a spider at the centre of its web, stands the corpse-man from the British Museum, Baron Ausbach. He gloats over a prone human figure strapped to an operating table.

'Soon,' he croons, 'Harold Lathers will be no more. I shall extract the essence of your life-force for my own power and confer on your body the gift of perpetual animation!' The evil Baron reaches towards a control panel which seems to control his infernal machinery . . .

Will you descend the stairs to aid Harold Lathers? Turn to **334**. Or will you leap at the ancient chandelier which hangs from the lofty ceiling? Turn to **238**.

212

With a long sigh, you sink to the floor. The succubus descends upon you with a peculiar sucking noise. Later, it rises and boils back into the curious seventeenth-century painting above the mantelpiece. Below, your body lies drained of all moisture like an unwrapped Egyptian mummy. So ends your adventure.

Thoth's strange voice echoes round the chamber.

'The pyramidion is a crystal, fashioned by a race known as the Polyps of Ombos. It is a power focus, or key, used to draw matter from one dimension to another. It was Het who ensured that the Polyps brought it to this world, in the hopes that she could then use it as a gateway, but her plans were foiled when the Polyps and their creature-ship were buried beneath the rocks of North Wales.

'Thus the crystal was lost for millions of years, until the Egyptian Pharaoh, Khefu, stumbled upon it in the course of his sorcerous experiments. He cast potent spells to draw it through time and space to his palace and, in so doing, he attracted the powers of the Outer Darkness. Thus Het learned of the crystal's rediscovery and, working through it, she corrupted Khefu. She commanded him to build this,' Thoth waves his hand in the air, 'the first pyramid, in imitation of the pyramidion, so that a gateway to the underworld could be opened. Then she instructed Khefu to focus the crystal, so she could use it to control the very fabric of the earth, which belongs to the primeval beast, Crom Cruach. But Khefu died before all the necessary ceremonies could be completed and, with his death, the spells that held the crystal were broken and it slipped back to its tomb beneath the hills of Wales.

'Frustrated yet again, Het collapsed back into the Outer Darkness to brood. She returned to place Ausbach on its trail. Even now, he is within reach of achieving her ultimate aim! You must act swiftly to thwart her plans.'

If you have the khephera sword, turn to **248**. Otherwise, turn to **270**.

Your bolt bursts inside the Baron's skull. He staggers forward clutching his head, then his legs buckle and he topples into the pit of time! You have destroyed Ausbach at last! But the effort has cost you 3 points of Endurance. Suddenly, you feel the ground pulse beneath your feet, the pillars of the stone circle begin to sway and a chill seizes your body, as you sense a malign intelligence questing for your life. A nebulous haze begins to form in the centre of the pillar of fire and a hideous outline forms within it! You must act swiftly to close the gateway. Your only hope is to destroy the pyramidion that still glows on the altar. But how?

Will you use Thoth's mace? Turn to **342**. The khephera sword, knobkerrie or swordstick? Turn to **355**. Or will you snatch the pyramidion from the altar and hurl it into the pit? Turn to **224**.

For what seems a long time, you experience the unpleasant sensation of falling through a great soggy darkness. Then suddenly, you materialise a few feet above a thatched roof. Moments later, you extricate yourself from the wreckage and stagger through an open door into the night. You have lost 1 point of Endurance.

Harold Lathers stands without, nursing a bump on his head.

'I don't understand,' he says. 'This isn't the black room at Shadwick House, nor even the grounds. We seem to have emerged in some kind of village, but it's as quiet as the grave.'

You fumble in your pocket and draw out the electric torch. Its beam shines wanly as you return to the small silent cottage. The pale light reveals a grisly sight. You fell through the roof on to a bed which bears a desiccated grinning corpse! You hurry Harold away, down a narrow street bounded on either side by small silent cottages. You are sure that behind every door lies a grisly grinning secret.

To what dark domain has Ausbach's infernal gateway brought you? Turn to **239**.

216

The strange pulsating pattern seems horribly attractive. You feel compelled to reach out and run your hands across the cold luminous surface. As you do so, your hands plunge beneath the surface into an ice-cold liquid! You have lost 2 points of Endurance.

Desperately, you try to pull free of the table, but your hands seem to be encased within the marble! A numbing chill begins to creep up your arms and you feel a mad urge to immerse your body in the marble pool. You must act quickly to break the spell of the Dragon Table. Match your Strength against the Dragon Table's Strength (6) on the Conflict Table. If you succeed, turn to **276**. If you fail, turn to **295**.

Your boot crunches into the hand, crushing it into the floor. Brown dust floats up from around your boot and a disgusting smell fills the chamber. You have destroyed the Hand of Glory. Turning, you pass through the carved archway. Turn to **120**.

Petrie-Smith listens carefully to your account, then sits back in his armchair and gazes thoughtfully into the fire.

After a few minutes' meditation he turns to you and says, 'In Egyptian legend there are tales of sorcerers who travelled great distances in an instant, by means of magic "Thaati" gateways. They called it "flying on the wings of Horus". It sounds to me as if the thief, or his master, constructed such a gateway in the British Museum. However, he or they would require another, identical, gateway at the home base. I know of a sarcophagus which is the exact twin of the one you describe; it is part of the

collection of the Egyptologist, Sir Roderick Lathers, at Shandwick House in Kent. Tomorrow, I shall follow up my assertion in the British Museum Library, while you collect the tools needed for a trip to Shandwick House!' Turn to **236**.

219

You tug a battered navigational map from its stowage next to the dead pilot. His intended route is marked in red pencil: Zurich, Innsbruck, Salzburg, Lintz and on to Vienna. You check the compass: you are currently headed due north. Glancing at your watch, you estimate flying time and decide that you must be off course, with Munich somewhere to the north-west.

You bank the aircraft on to a north-westerly course, certain that you have left the hidden perils of the Alpine peaks behind. There seems to be sufficient fuel to reach your goal. A short while later, the rain eases and ahead you glimpse the distant lights of a city. Munich is approaching. The comforting lights remind you of the grisly corpse seated next to you. How could you possibly explain what has befallen you to the authorities? Will you radio ahead some plausible excuse? Turn to **181**. Or will you attempt a clandestine landing? Turn to **89**.

220

You have entered a large cabin with attached servant's quarters. The curtains are neatly drawn, the bedclothes unruffled. No clothes hang in the wardrobe, no personal belongings rest in the drawers. The same is true of the servant's room. The only sign of habitation is a large travelling trunk in the middle of the main cabin, and an antique object resting on the dressing table.

Will you examine the trunk? Turn to **182**. Or the table? Turn to **84**.

You draw your pistol, drop on one knee and open fire. The gun coughs once and stabs flame. Ausbach grips his head as if in agony, topples backwards over the handrail and rolls away to his doom over the side of the airship. (Deduct one bullet from your Character Profile.) You rise, pocket the pistol, then struggle back towards the service ladder.

As you make ready to descend back into the *Lucretia*, you glance upwards. The wind stifles your scream as a great winged beast plummets towards you, dressed in the tatters of a man's clothing! Powerful talons grip your shoulders and you are torn up and away from the world of men. Wild yellow eyes stare into your own and a vile familiar voice mocks you above the wind's howl.

'You are mine now. You shall be my slave and your life-force my toy!' Your mind slides into a thankful oblivion. Turn to **25**.

As the door swings back, you shine the torch across a library. Two window casements and a pair of heavy oak doors in the south wall are the only features which provide relief from the rows of leather-bound books, reports and files. A rich Persian carpet lies on the floor and below the west window stands a stately desk, covered with papers and a model of a pyramid.

Will you examine the desk? Turn to **284**. Or will you try the doors in the south wall? Turn to **325**.

You awake feeling exhausted and unable to move your limbs. Someone is leaning over you, holding a syringe.

You hear him say, 'Gentlemen, as you can see, the patient is quite calm now. You may ask your questions, Inspector.'

A thin, bespectacled and slightly balding man comes into

view. He smiles in a kindly way and pats you on the shoulder.

'Don't worry, you are in safe hands now. Perhaps you can tell me who you are and where you live?'

You would like to tell him, but the trouble is, you don't know who you are . . . This adventure is at an end.

224

Glowing with a luminous blue light, the pyramidion lies on top of the altar. Rushing forward, you grasp it with your hand and howl in pain. Its surface is red-hot and you have burned your hand. Lose 2 points of Stamina.

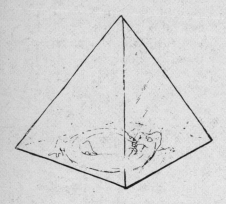

Roll against your Strength to see if you can hold the pyramidion long enough to cast it into the pit. If you succeed, turn to **305**. If you fail, turn to **324**.

225

Together, you and Harold slam the door. Luckily, the bolt is on your side. For a few moments you recover your breath, then head off along a dank corridor, lit by guttering reed torches. The way leads to the edge of a vast gloomy pit. Turn to **47**.

Thoth's voice fills the chamber.

'Ausbach may be slain in two ways. One is to turn the very element he serves – fire – against him. The other is to find his life-force, which Het has removed from his body and imprisoned somewhere in the underworld.'

If you now want to learn about the pyramidion, turn to **213**. If you do not and you have the khephera sword, turn to **248**. Otherwise, turn to **270**.

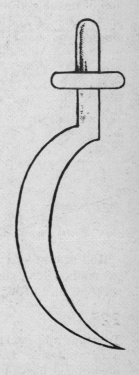

If you succeeded in your Mentality roll, you have lost 1 point of Endurance. If you failed the roll, you have lost 2 points of Endurance.

In disbelief you stand before the empty sarcophagus, the image of the corpse-man's grotesque face seared on your mind. You are roused from your trance by the sound of breaking glass. Turning, you see a mummy struggling free of its broken display case. Blindly, the ancient corpse gropes towards you. Its joints creak and a vile muffled whimpering escapes from its bandaged head.

Roll against your Mentality. If you succeed, turn to **242**. If you fail, turn to **266**.

If this is the second time you have failed your Mentality roll, turn to **115**.

228

Clutching your head, you crumple to the ground. Greedily, the ka falls on top of you, its talons digging into your back. This is the end of the adventure for you.

229

You thrust the fire-brand into the creature's jaws. With a long, drawn-out, hissing sound, the creature erupts into a ball of flame! The explosion knocks you back upon the sand, causing 2 points' damage to your Stamina.

Struggling to your feet, you turn to see Petrie-Smith finishing another of the creatures. His gunfire tears great wounds in the creature's hide and a noisome liquid pours out. The toad-thing shrivels, crumples, then sags into a slimy membrane upon the desert sand. Turn to **201**.

230

Your attack smashes the creature's body. Its odious screams become a long gurgling sigh. Its legs collapse and it slowly rolls off the dead pilot.

You hurry aft, collect a mail bag and fling it over the corpse. Then you scrape up the vile bundle and toss it into the plane's fuselage. Now you must try to fly the aircraft.

If you fired five or more bullets during the battle, turn to **287**. If you fired less, or beat the creature with the fire extinguisher alone, turn to **372**.

231

Can you dodge past the creature and strike off its sting? Match your Dexterity against the terracotta scorpion's Dexterity (8). If you succeed, turn to **79**.

If you fail, the creature attacks! It will first try to seize you in its claws. Roll against its Dexterity. If it succeeds, turn to **173**.

If the creature fails, you may try to complete this daring scheme. Return and repeat the first paragraph of this section. Otherwise, you may try to escape. Turn to **281**. Or draw your pistol. Turn to **264**. Or pipe upon the dragon whistle. Turn to **200**.

232

The strange pulsating pattern seems horribly attractive. You feel compelled to reach out and run your hands across the cold luminous surface. As you do so, your hands sink through the surface into an ice-cold liquid! With a gasp you draw back, pulling your hands free of the enchanted table. You have lost 1 point of Endurance.

Convinced of the Dragon Table's diabolical properties, you flee from the room. In the corridor you can turn north, turn to **172**. Or you can open the door in the east wall, turn to **138**.

233

The serpent man proves to be too agile and strong an opponent. Gradually, he wears you down. Finally, exhausted and bloody, your guard slips and the creature springs at your throat. Sharp fangs puncture your skin, injecting a cold tingling poison. Your legs sag, but the creature supports you under the arms. As your mind drifts towards oblivion, you hear the scaly creature speaking to you.

'My master will be pleased,' it rasps. 'For I have vanquished his only human foe.' Then darkness fills your mind. This adventure is at an end for you.

234

You are too slow! The hand of fire catches you as you grasp the jar, enveloping you in flames. You cry out in agony and another's cry joins yours. Then your flaming body is swept

off the ground towards the pit of time.

You have failed to close the gateway, but you have destroyed Ausbach. The flames that consumed you have consumed his life-force as well! Your adventure ends here.

235

Your attempt to pick this door lock is a dismal failure. So will you now attempt to force the door? Turn to **255**. Will you visit the cabin of the mysterious American instead? Turn to **78**. Or will you abandon the investigation and return to your own cabin? Turn to **45**.

236

You awake in the morning refreshed and eager for action. (Once again you may recover half of any lost Stamina or Endurance.) Petrie-Smith has already left for the British Museum, so you breakfast alone and then start planning your trip to Shandwick House.

Rummaging through the drawers of your writing desk, you discover an Ordnance Survey map of southern England. Spreading the map over the table, you search for Shandwick House and find it located close to the village of Gorham, about twenty miles from London. It seems prudent to make a nocturnal visit. Abandoning the map, you hurry into town to gather equipment. From a locksmith you buy a skeleton key, while a hardware shop furnishes you with a powerful electric torch. Note these two items on your Character Profile under Possessions.

Back at home, you open the safe in the study wall and remove your automatic pistol. Enter the following details on your Character Profile under Weapons: Automatic Pistol 2D6/–. The pistol holds nine bullets. Note them under the Possessions section of the Character Profile. Each time you successfully shoot a target, you will cause damage to its Stamina equivalent to the roll of two dice (2D6). Try to keep this weapon with you at all times. You will be told when it is possible to reload.

As dusk falls you leave Bedford Terrace. Will you drive straight to Shandwick House? Turn to **274**. Or will you visit Gorham first to question the locals? Turn to **258**.

237

You deal the dog man a blow with your chosen weapon. Roll against your Dexterity. If you succeed, deduct your weapon's damage from the creature's Stamina. If the dog man is slain, turn to **58**.

If the creature survives, he will continue the struggle. Roll against the dog man's Dexterity of 8. If he succeeds, his mace will smash 2 points from your Stamina. If you are reduced to zero, turn to **132**.

If you survive, you can continue this combat by repeating the first paragraph of this section. Otherwise, you could draw your pistol. Turn to **202**. Or you could try to escape. Turn to **177**.

238

Boldly, you climb upon the balcony rail, then launch yourself through space towards the chandelier. You hope your leap will carry you across the hall to where Ausbach stands. Roll against your Dexterity. If you succeed, turn to **251**. If you fail, turn to **278**.

239

At last you step out of the narrow silent street into what appears to be a main thoroughfare. Instantly, you are dazzled by the lights of a lorry. The vehicle grinds to a halt and a tall Arab, dressed in khaki with a red fez upon his head, greets you.

'My friends, it is not seemly for visitors to Cairo to stroll after dark in our village of the dead.'

Hurriedly, you concoct a story for the policeman's benefit, then humbly ask for directions to the Grand Hotel, where Petrie-Smith may still be staying. Turn to **257**.

240

Lifting your foot, you stamp down at the hand but it scampers away from the shadow you cast and clambers on to your other foot. Horrified by its agility, you feel it scurry up your leg and across your chest. Cold fingers curl round your throat! Roll against the hand's Strength (8). If it succeeds, it will crush 2 points of Stamina from your body. If this reduces you to zero, turn to **254**. However, if it fails, you can try to tear it from your throat by matching your Strength against the hand's Strength on the Conflict Table. If you succeed, turn to **273**. If you fail, turn to **300**.

241

With heart pounding, you pull back on the steering column with one hand and advance the throttles, to give the engines more power, with the other. The plane responds, pulling out of its dive of death, back on to a level flight path.

The crisis has brought the plane below the clouds and into a rain storm. Visibility is poor – at any moment you may fly into a mountainside. You must also find out where you are. You reach for the pilot's flight plan. Turn to **219**.

242

You have lost 1 point of Endurance. Now, how will you defend yourself against this animated corpse? Will you fight with your swordstick? Turn to **22**. Or your knobkerrie? Turn to **6**. Or will you flee from the museum? Turn to **82**.

243

'Fool!' screams the cold confident voice above the storm. 'No mortal can stand against me.' Both Ausbach's arms shoot out towards you and a web of scintillating blue electricity arcs through space to embrace you. The plasma bursts across your chest and propels you over the handrail. You roll away to your doom over the side of the airship.

Down, down into the depths of the sky you plunge. Your breath is torn away on the wind, your body buffeted over and over. You lose 2 points of Endurance as your mind slides into a thankful oblivion. Turn to **25**.

244

You have lost 1 point of Endurance.

'Yes, my friend,' says the Colonel. 'Once I was beguiled by Het's dark power. I paid the price. And Baron Ausbach is a living corpse.'

He rises and shows you to the cabin door. Will you now visit Ausbach's cabin? Turn to **192**. Or will you abandon the investigation and return to your cabin? Turn to **338**.

245

This hallway only runs for a short distance before terminating in a large window which overlooks the gardens. There is a locked door in the east wall marked Lumber Room and there is another door in the west wall. Will you open this door? Turn to **222**. Will you return to the landing to try the double doors? Turn to **325**. Or will you explore the south hallway? Turn to **204**.

246

As you rise from your seat, the aircraft lurches. You struggle forward to the cabin door only to find it bolted shut on the inside. You hammer on the wood and call for the pilot to open up. In reply, blood trickles under the door frame. You are alone, with only the mad beat of the engines for company. Will you try to force the cabin door? Turn to **203**. Or will you remain where you are? Turn to **186**.

247

As the hunchback prepares to strike another blow, you leap forward and block his cleaver arm, then swing the candleholder down on to his twisted frame. Roll 2D6. If the result is 7 or more, turn to **184**. If it is less, you inflict 2 points of damage to the hunchback's Stamina (15), then turn to **209**.

Thoth views the khephera warily. Then he speaks.

'That sword will be of use to you against the shades of the underworld, but it has an evil history and should be used with caution.'

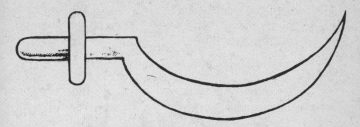

He hands you a small gold coin and gestures towards the gilded door.

'That door leads to the ferry, and the ferryman will require payment.' As Thoth speaks, he fades away and you are left to pass through the door. Turn to **160**.

249

In the presence of the ka, the khephera glows with a deadly white sheen, for it was forged specifically to slay the spirits of the underworld. As the ka spots the blade, an inhuman cry of anger bursts from its throat and it tries to wheel away. Swinging the sword in a wide arc, you cut up towards the ka's belly. Roll against your Dexterity. If you succeed, turn to **367**. If you fail, turn to **357**.

250

You find yourself standing at the top of a massive stairwell, which descends down into an unfathomable pit. A cold wind rises from the depths. It chills your body and bears a most disturbing animal odour. Every sense warns you to run from the chasm, for you know that something terrible is rising in the darkness.

Now you see movement below. A woman is climbing towards you, her arms outstretched in welcome. Yet something is wrong with her gait and appearance. She has the body of a woman, but the chiselled features of a snake.

A few steps below you, the creature halts and a vile, cold, sibilant voice calls to you. 'Come down into the pit, come down from the realm of men into the realm of Het.'

The adventure is at an end for you.

251

Your hands lock round the chandelier's frame and the momentum of your dive carries you across the hall. Judging the moment perfectly, you let go of the creaking chandelier and plummet down on to Ausbach. He grunts and collapses in a senseless heap on the flagstones.

Turning, you rush to the table and begin to fumble with the leather thongs that bind the young man to the table. Weakly, he struggles upright and introduces himself as Sir Roderick Lathers' son, Harold.

'Come,' he says. 'I think I know how to escape from this laboratory.' He leads you down a hall into a gloomy corridor, lit by guttering reed torches. It brings you to the edge of a vast pit. Turn to **47**.

252

This unexpected transformation has cost you 2 points of Endurance. You watch in stunned horror as the creature peels the maidservant's gloves from its sharply taloned hands. Then the creature pounces.

Roll against the serpent man's Dexterity (9). If he succeeds, his talons slash 2 points from your Stamina. If you are reduced to zero, turn to **233**. If not, read on.

Now it is your turn to attack. Roll against your Dexterity. If you succeed, the dagger cuts 2 points from the creature's Stamina. If your attack slays the creature, turn to **279**.

If the serpent man still lives, he will strike back. Return and repeat the second paragraph of this section. The battle proceeds in this way until one of you is slain.

253

As you struggle to free yourself from the clutches of this corpse-creature, you feel a chill begin to creep through your body. Contact with the mummy seems to be draining you of strength. Can you free yourself before it is too late?

Match your Strength −1 against the mummy's Strength (8 + 1) on the Conflict Table. If you fail to break the mummy's hold, you must repeat this section, but this time add another point to the mummy's Strength and reduce your Strength by 1 point. The struggle proceeds in this way until your Strength falls to zero, or you manage to get free. Turn to **131**.

If you succeed in breaking the mummy's grip, you can fight on with the swordstick, turn to **26**. Or with the knobkerrie, turn to **74**. Or you can try to escape, turn to **82**.

(If you lose Strength you must play further sections at the reduced level until you are given recovery instructions.)

254

Denied air by the skeletal terror clutched about your neck, you fall choking into the dust of the chamber floor. Your desperate spasms grow feeble and finally you expire. As you pass beyond life, you seem to hear a mocking voice calling from a great distance.

'I knew your meddling curiosity would be your downfall!' The adventure is over for you.

255

To break into the room, you must pit your Strength against the door's Strength (6) on the Conflict Table. If you succeed, the door lock bursts open and you plunge into the cabin. Turn to **220**. If you fail, you can try once more, but if you fail a second time, you must proceed to **275**.

256

Returning to Bedford Terrace, you find Petrie-Smith toasting crumpets over the parlour fire. He invites you to join him and, while you eat (regain 1 point of Stamina), he listens to your tale.

By the time you have finished, the fire has burned down to a red glow and the corners of the room are hidden in shadow. Petrie-Smith's chair creaks as he shifts his weight and then he begins to speak.

'I spent the day following up my assertions about the Thaati gateway and Het the Destroyer. Het is an Egyptian deity associated with the undead, such as ghouls, zombies and vampires, and the element of fire. Few myths mention her, but those that do state that she dwells in the Outer

Darkness and is a threat to the world. Thaati gateways are specifically connected with those sorcerers who chose to worship Het; so too is the symbol of the serpent devouring its own tail.

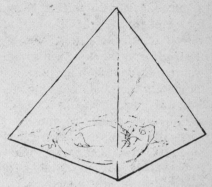

'The Egyptians called this symbol the "Binding of Apep". They believed it was a talisman created by the sorcerer-pharaoh Khefu to help Het gain control of the element of earth as well as fire. If Het had been able to use the talisman, she could have destroyed the world, but before Khefu could give it to her, he was killed and the talisman was lost. The same legend also states that the spells which activate the talisman and summon Het may only be cast in the underworld.

'At first I thought this information all but useless, but with your discoveries it takes on a new and fearsome light. Ausbach must know of the pyramidion's powers and he has stolen it to gain access to the underworld – and for what reason other than to summon Het and to activate the talisman which lies encased within the crystal? Why he should want to do this, I do not know. Perhaps he is mad, or a servant of Het, but whatever the case, his actions threaten to place the world in grave danger and we must stop him!

'Tonight we will rest. But in the morning you must fly after the airship *Lucretia* in your plane, whilst I shall book a passage to Cairo to investigate the pyramid of Khefu.' Turn to **369**.

257

You awake in one of the hotel's plush bedrooms. You have recovered half of any Stamina and Endurance lost in yesterday's encounters. If your Mentality was impaired, this has returned to normal. After a hearty breakfast, which gives you another point of Stamina, you seek out Petrie-Smith and Harold Lathers.

'I was intrigued to hear,' says Petrie-Smith, 'of your unorthodox mode of transport and your ultimate destination. Perhaps this Ausbach fellow has a sense of humour? Now, come to the window, both of you.' Your old friend leads you to a table, on which is spread an archaeological survey map.

'As you can see,' he says, 'Khefu's pyramid lies only a few miles from Cairo. I have hired a number of native guides and their camels, so we can be there by nightfall. You have been singularly unable to defeat this Ausbach by physical battle, so I have formulated a plan which depends only upon guile. Tonight, the moon completes its cycle. You will recall from the Hymn to Het, discovered in Shandwick House, that this is the best time for her servants to enter the underworld. Well, I am certain that Ausbach will try to enter the pyramid tonight to perform his unspeakable rites. We need only wait until he passes into the underworld, then we can recover your pyramidion!' The sage old man slaps the table in triumph.

'But how will stealing this pyramidion defeat Ausbach?' inquires Harold.

'My dear fellow,' replies Petrie-Smith, almost tetchily. 'The pyramidion is some kind of key which opens the dimensions. If we steal it while Ausbach is in the underworld, he will be trapped for good, entombed with the vile goddess he serves! Now, come along, the both of

you. Gather your equipment, for we leave within the hour.'

You take this time as an opportunity to clean your pistol and reload its magazine. Turn to **277**.

258

Gorham is an old village whose buildings cluster round a large pond. It has one public house, The Crooked Staff, and it is this building you park outside. Opening the door, you enter a small oak-beamed bar which smells of beer and is warmed by a small fire. Two villagers are leaning against the bar and a third, who looks like a gamekeeper, is sitting near the fire. Will you offer to buy the locals a drink? Turn to **290**. Or will you just buy one for yourself and hope that the villagers' curiosity will lead them to speak to you? Turn to **306**.

259

The assassin-bug leaps and crashes on to your chest. Several pairs of its legs seek to pinion your arms, as it opens its jaws to reveal rows of jagged fangs. Roll against the creature's Dexterity (8). If it succeeds, turn to **271**. If it fails, turn to **298**.

260

You hurtle through the air and smash into Ausbach, knocking him off his feet. He somersaults back over the altar and, with a scream, falls into the pit. Crawling to the edge, you peer over and see his body spinning down through the flames, then the smoke and heat force you to turn away. You have destroyed Ausbach at last!

A hissing noise draws your eyes back to the pillar of fire. Emerging from a nebulous haze that writhes at its centre is a monstrous snake head. You must act swiftly to close the gateway Ausbach has opened. Your only hope is to destroy the pyramidion. But how?

Will you use Thoth's mace? Turn to **342**. The khephera sword, knobkerrie or swordstick? Turn to **355**. The dragon whistle? Turn to **319**. Or will you snatch the pyramidion from the altar and hurl it into the pit? Turn to **224**.

261

You descend the great staircase and unbolt the front door. Outside the rain has stopped and the clouds have dispersed. The waning moon casts a baleful silver light across the shrubbery. Slipping your torch into a pocket, you crunch boldly along the gravel drive. Suddenly, a cry goes up in the woods to your right. Looking behind, you see a figure emerge from the trees, then a puff of smoke appears and the foliage next to you is peppered with shot. You have disturbed the gamekeeper! Turning on your heels, you run for the safety of the public road. Turn to **256**.

262

You suddenly feel certain that the tripod, which stands next to the Guardian's dais, may hold the key to your survival. However, the dog man stands between you and your goal. Can you dodge past him? Match your Dexterity against the dog man's Dexterity (8) on the Conflict Table. If you succeed, turn to **153**.

If you fail, the dog man blocks your move and strikes with his mace. Roll against the creature's Dexterity. If it succeeds, you suffer the loss of 2 points of Stamina. If you are reduced to zero, turn to **132**.

If you live, will you try to complete your stratagem? Repeat the first paragraph of this section. Otherwise, you could battle on with the khephera sword, Thoth's mace, your knobkerrie or your swordstick. Turn to **237**. You could draw your pistol. Turn to **202**. Or you could try to escape. Turn to **177**.

263

This weird vision has cost you 1 point of Endurance. Now you must act for mankind, sanity and science. Will you draw your pistol? Turn to **221**. Hold on high Petrie-Smith's blue crystal scarab? Turn to **183**. Cast the warrior's wand? Turn to **126**. Or play upon the dragon whistle? Turn to **108**.

264

You may fire one, two or three bullets. Roll against your Dexterity each time you fire, for accuracy. Total the damage and deduct it from the creature's Stamina. Strike the bullets you have fired from your Character Profile. If you slay the creature, turn to **100**.

If the creature survives, it attacks! The terracotta scorpion will try to seize you in its claws. Roll against its Dexterity (8). If it succeeds, turn to **173**.

If the creature fails, you are able to counter-attack. If you still have bullets, you can return and repeat the first paragraph of this section. Otherwise, you can try either to run away. Turn to **281**. Or you can use your knobkerrie or your swordstick. Turn to **231**. Or you can pipe upon the dragon whistle. Turn to **200**.

You have lost 2 points of Endurance.

'Yes, my friend,' says the Colonel. 'Once I was beguiled by Het's dark power – and paid the price.' He laughs the cold mirthless laugh of one haunted by a terrible secret. The laughter rolls around the cabin and you gaze into those vile snake eyes. You lurch backwards, grip the door handle and stumble from the cabin.

Will you gather your wits and set off to investigate Ausbach's cabin? Turn to **192**. Or will you abandon the investigation and return to your own cabin? Turn to **338**.

You have lost 2 points of Endurance and the mummy is upon you! Match the mummy's Dexterity (6) against your Dexterity on the Conflict Table. If the mummy succeeds,

turn to **280**. If it fails, will you fight with your swordstick? Turn to **22**. Or with your knobkerrie? Turn to **6**. Or will you flee from the museum? Turn to **82**.

The creature lurches at you and tries to gobble you into its noisome maw. Its teeth snare your arm and you are poised on the edge of its sag-belly! Match your Strength against the toad-thing's Strength (8) on the Conflict Table. If you succeed, you tear free from the creature and can counter-attack either with the pistol. Turn to **332**. Or with the fire-brand. Turn to **229**. If you fail, turn to **341**.

Can you escape through the archway door and slam it in the face of the bogie horde? Match your Dexterity against the creatures' combined Dexterity (9) on the Conflict Table. If you succeed, turn to **225**. If you fail, how will you defend yourself now? With corpse dust? Turn to **207**. Your pistol? Turn to **180**. Or your bare fists? Turn to **169**.

*269

As you advance, the slope grows steeper, the air warmer and the pink glow thickens to a curious red. Ahead a great circle of monoliths rears out of the ground. Passing between two of the standing stones, you have to shield your eyes; you are looking upon a vast pit which glows with a demonic light.

You have found the pit of time. Framed against its edge, Ausbach stands before an altar on which lies the pyramidion. He is chanting in a harsh guttural tongue. Even as you watch, his chanting reaches a frenzied peak, he flings his arms in the air and a pillar of fire roars out of the pit. You must act quickly, for Ausbach has just opened a gateway to the Outer Darkness. At any moment Het the Destroyer will enter the underworld. Rushing from the cover of the stones, you charge towards Ausbach.

If you have the jar containing his life-force, turn to **199**. If you wish to challenge him with the crocodile cap, turn to **140**. Otherwise, knowing he is immune to any normal weapons, you resolve to hurl him into the pillar of fire. Turn to **125**.

270

From out of the air, Thoth plucks a stone mace and hands it to you, saying, 'With this, you shall beat down the shades of the underworld.'

As you clasp the cold stone, energy pulses into your body

and you regain 2 points of Endurance. Enter the mace on your Character Profile: Mace of Thoth 4/4. When you use the mace, roll against your Dexterity. If you succeed, the weapon strikes 4 points from the Stamina or Endurance of your enemies.

Finally, Thoth hands you a small gold coin and gestures towards a door at the back of the room.

'That door leads to the ferry and the ferryman will require payment.' Turn to **160**.

271

'Die!' hisses the assassin-bug and sinks its fangs into your neck. In a few moments the assassin-bug has completed its hideous work. Your lifeless body crashes to the floor. The adventure is over for you.

Your bolt is powerful, but misdirected. Ausbach spins round, a look of fear and fury on his obscene face.

'Fool! That cap is dedicated to Yehog and, with the gateway open, you are bound to have attracted his attention!' Even as Ausbach talks, you are losing consciousness. A feeling of vertigo overwhelms you, the ground seems to swim round your feet and you fall.

The last you remember is a malign intelligence enveloping you, before your life is sucked away. This is the end of the adventure for you.

Working your fingers under the withered flesh, you prise the Hand of Glory off. It writhes in your grip, vile blisters bubble up on its skin and, without warning, it explodes in a cloud of disgusting dust!

Choking, you stumble back, inadvertently inhaling the dust which carries the spores of a virulent virus. From now on, until you are cured or die, you will lose 1 point of Stamina every time you turn to an even-numbered entry in this adventure. Note this effect on your Character Profile.

Coughing, you pick up your lantern and stumble through the carved doorway. Turn to **120**.

A mile or so down the road, you spot a sign for Shandwick House and a pair of imposing, wrought iron gates. You park the car in the shadow of the estate's ivy-clad wall and hurry back.

The bolt slides back easily enough, but the gates protest on rusty hinges as you push them open. You step out into the dark shadows of the gravel drive. Unkempt rhododendron bushes and gnarled trees line your route. They fill the night with a disquieting rustling mutter as you pick your way between puddles and fallen branches. The drive opens out to reveal the forbidding prospect of Shandwick House, a great mansion built in the weird gothic style of the mid-nineteenth century. As you plunge into the dark shadow of the place, you feel quite alone and imagine that furtive eyes keep watch from the unlit rooms. Stealthily, you approach the front door and peer in through the letter box. An old suit of armour stands to one side of the door, opposite is a hat and coat stand, the rest of the hallway is lost in gloom. Maybe there is some easier and more secluded entrance to the place?

Will you investigate the south side of the house? Turn to 95. Or will you explore the north side? Turn to 320.

275

As you struggle with the door, you receive a sharp tap on your shoulder. Instantly, you take your weight off the door and sheepishly turn to face the airship's Purser, flanked by two stewards.

'I think you ought to come and sample the accommodation in my brig,' he says. 'It seems your flight is over.' So is this adventure.

276

With a mighty heave, you topple the Dragon Table. Your hands are free, the hideous illusion broken. The bronze box scatters its contents across the floor and an acrid sickly smoke begins to fill the room. Shivering, you beat a hasty retreat from the black room and slam the door behind you.

Back in the corridor, you feel a sense of life and well-being flood through your body. You have recovered 1 point of Endurance. Will you now continue north along the corridor? Turn to **172**. Or will you try the door opposite in the east wall? Turn to **138**.

277

Despite Petrie-Smith's enthusiasm, travel in the heat of the Egyptian day is not advisable. You reach the crumbled splendour of Khefu's pyramid at sunset, after an uncomfortable and fly-blown journey. However, a hearty meal eaten around a blazing camp fire soon revives your spirits and gives you 1 point of Stamina. The meal over, you set a guard to watch over the pyramid's entrance, then settle down to await moon-rise. Not long afterwards, the attack begins.

You are sitting with your back to the pyramid, watching one of the Egyptian porters patrolling the camel lines. Suddenly, the man seems to double up, as if in pain. Through the still night air, you hear a strange gobbling noise and the man disappears from view! Calling to Petrie-Smith, you pull a burning brand from the fire and run to the spot. There is no sign of the porter, but the sand is pockmarked with strange circular depressions.

'Most curious,' whispers Petrie-Smith. 'And look, the camels seem untroubled.'

Then, nearby, you hear a disturbing slopping noise and a monstrous toad-thing lumbers at you out of the dark. Roll against your Mentality. If you succeed, turn to **299**. If you fail, turn to **315**.

278

Your leap is ill-judged; you gain a tenuous grip upon the chandelier's frame, but have no momentum to carry you across the hall. Only one option is left to you: to drop to the floor some fifteen feet below. Roll against your Dexterity. If you succeed, turn to **291**. If you fail, turn to **318**.

Throughout this battle the creature has been silent. Now, at last, it groans. It staggers. A forked tongue flickers. Then the reptile man sags against you, slips sideways and crashes to the floor. Green blood oozes from his many wounds. Disgusted, you turn away and make for the door. If you examined the serpent glass, you may choose to take it with you. Enter it under Possessions on your Character Profile. Turn to **338**.

280

The mummy flings its arms around your body, pinioning your arms. You are trapped, with your face pressed hard against the corpse-thing's brittle wrappings, unless you can break its grip.

Match your Strength against the mummy's unnatural Strength (8). If you fail to break the mummy's grip, turn to **253**. If you succeed in struggling free, you can fight on with the swordstick, turn to **26**. Or with the knobkerrie, turn to **74**. Or you can try to escape, turn to **82**.

281

Somehow, you must evade the scorpion. Turning on your heels, you run away through the cavern, with the creature in hot pursuit. The light from your lantern swings crazily across the cavern wall as you search for an exit. You find it in a narrow cleft in the cavern wall, through which the scorpion could not possibly follow. Desperately, you scramble up towards the narrow gap, but can you evade the creature's final lunge?

Match your Dexterity against the scorpion's Dexterity (8) on the Conflict Table. If you succeed, you manage to slip through the cleft. Turn to **130**. If you fail, turn to **110**.

282

You call to the pilot down the voice tube, then press your ear to the mechanism for his reply. There is none yet, behind the measured throb of the engines, you distinctly hear a horrid gurgling sigh. It is time to go forward and investigate. Turn to **246**.

283

You have lost 2 points of Endurance. The dog man raises his muzzle and sniffs; his eyes roll back and his lips curl. A vicious snarl rends the air as the creature leaps at you. He is armed with a dog-headed mace and has a Stamina of 14. Note this on your Character Profile.

The mace flashes through the air towards your body. Roll against the dog man's Dexterity (8). If he succeeds, you have 2 points smashed from your Stamina. If you are reduced to zero, turn to **132**.

If he fails, you can fight on. Will you use the khephera sword, Thoth's mace, your knobkerrie or your swordstick? Turn to **237**. Your pistol? Turn to **202**. Or you could try to escape. Turn to **177**.

284

A sign let into the model's base declares this to be a representation of 'The Pyramid of Khefu'. Beside the model is a large crumpled sheet of paper and a small brown envelope. The paper is illustrated with a representation of a hieroglyphic text, beneath which is a translation written in a spidery cramped style:

Discovered in the second chamber within the pyramid of

Khefu. A papyrus of Amon-Khet, Chief Priest of the deity Het. Translated by Baron Ausbach.

'. . . when the moon hath passed its glory and fades in the east, take thee the crystal pyramidion from the hands of Horus, in the great pyramid of Khefu. Then pass through into the Hall of Entry. Abase thyself and pour out thy preparations, chanting these words with the tongue of the serpent, unto the glory of those who dwell in the Outer Darkness:

> Het, I cry to thee, destroyer!
> Avert the terror of Yehog!
> Avert the wrath of Thoth!
> Bind thee the coils of Apep,
> He who serves thee in darkness.
>
> Dissolve these walls
> So I may enter the caverns of dust,
> The halls of silence,
> The realm of torment,
> Where only thy servants may tread.'

Beneath the text is a drawing of the crystal key – the pyramidion stolen from your house!

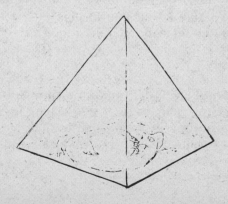

Now you examine the brown envelope. Inside is a receipt for two airship tickets. The receipt was issued at Croydon aerodrome for the Paris, Vienna, Budapest and Constantinople flight of the airship *Lucretia*. The airship left Croydon early this evening. Deducing that the pyramidion's thief may be aboard the airship, you resolve to leave Shandwick House and return to London. You pocket the paper and the airship receipt. (Note this entry number on your Character Profile as Papyrus, in case you wish to read it again, but remember to take note of your current position if you do!) Then you leave the house. Turn to **261**.

285

You remove the cork stopper and empty the contents of the phial down your throat. The effect is instantaneous and startling. First, you feel a burning sensation in your chest and a feeling of breathlessness overwhelms you. Then a warm glow radiates through your body and you regain the roll of two six-sided dice to your Stamina (always remembering your Stamina may never exceed the total you began the adventure with).

However, there is a price to pay for using this unnatural aid. The crystals are unstable and may deteriorate at any time. Hereafter, whenever you turn to an entry marked with an * deduct 2 points of Stamina from your current rating. Now return to the relevant section in the adventure, having noted the above effect on your Character Profile.

286

You pull Ausbach sharply forward and he topples over you into the pit! But his long fingers clutch tightly to your jacket and, to your horror, you are pulled over with him! With a scream, you tumble into the pit of time and the flames surge up to consume both you and the Baron. This is the end of the adventure for you.

287

You ease yourself into the co-pilot's seat and grab the steering column. It feels horribly slack. Some of your bullets must have destroyed vital controls. Around you, the plane's fuselage begins to vibrate and the engines whine to fever pitch. Suddenly, you are through the clouds and plunging down towards the white world below. There is nothing you can do. The adventure is at an end.

288

Your gunfire rips into the toad-thing's hide and a noxious liquid pours from its wounds. The monster begins to shrivel, to collapse in upon itself. In a few moments nothing remains but a translucent membrane, draped over the figure of the drowned Egyptian porter.

You turn to see Petrie-Smith thrust a fire-brand into another toad-thing's maw. There is a hissing noise, then the creature erupts in a ball of flame. The explosion knocks the brave old man to the ground, but you are relieved to see him struggle to his feet a few moments later, unharmed. Turn to **201**.

*289

Gradually, the ground begins to rise and you pass among hundreds of crude stone pillars. Some are arranged in circles, others in line, but the bulk seem to be scattered at random across the landscape. A weird pink light illuminates the skyline ahead and you know instinctively that your arch-enemy, Ausbach, is nearby. Turn to **269**.

290

Your offer is greeted with cold stares and silence.

Then the gamekeeper speaks. 'There's none in Gorham that's so hard up they can't afford a drink. We've no need for strangers' money.'

Realising you have somehow offended them, you finish your drink quickly and return to the car. Turn to **274**.

291

You fall heavily, but skilfully manage to roll on your side and so lessen the shock. You have lost 1 point of Stamina.

'Curse your resourcefulness!' screams Ausbach. 'I have more important matters to attend to than your destruction. I leave you both to my pets!' Thrusting the table towards you, he flees from the hall.

You fumble with the leather thongs that bind the young man. Weakly, he struggles free, introducing himself as Sir Roderick Lathers' son, Harold.

'I fear we can expect no mercy from Ausbach's pets,' he says. 'They are the result of his vile experiments – the living dead and the never-to-be-born! Look! Even now they come, slavering for our blood!'

Into the hall slithers, hops and staggers a pack of jibbering bogies. Some cavort on stunted bird-like legs, others pull unspeakable serpent-like bodies across the flagstones. They smack their thin decayed lips and an evil expectant gleam lights their eyes.

Roll against your Mentality. If you succeed, turn to **358**. If you fail, turn to **373**.

292

You lose 2 points of Endurance as you gaze at this terror. This is no freak of nature, but a clay model animated by sorcery to defend Khefu's pyramid. The creature has a Stamina of 12. Note this on your Character Profile.

The terracotta scorpion clatters forward to attack. First, it will try to seize you in its claws. Roll against the creature's Dexterity (8). If it succeeds, turn to **173**. If it fails, how will you do battle? Draw your pistol? Turn to **264**. Use your knobkerrie or your swordstick? Turn to **231**. Or pipe upon the dragon whistle? Turn to **200**.

293

You dive for the jar, but will you be able to pull the brain out and destroy it before the flaming hand grabs you? Roll against your Dexterity. If you succeed, turn to **166**. If you fail, turn to **234**.

294

You have lost 1 point of Endurance. The dog man raises his muzzle in the air and sniffs; his eyes roll back and his lips curl. A vicious snarl rends the air as the creature leaps at you. He is armed with a dog-headed mace and has a Stamina of 14. Note this on your Character Profile.

How will you defend yourself against this abomination? If you have these weapons, you could use either the crocodile cap. Turn to **262**. Or the khephera sword, Thoth's mace, your knobkerrie or your swordstick. Turn to **237**. Otherwise, you could draw your pistol. Turn to **202**. Or you could try to escape. Turn to **177**.

295

You are unable to overcome the Dragon Table, which seems to be sucking your life-force from your body. Lose 2 points of Endurance. If you are reduced to zero, turn to **250**.

Desperately, you try to wrench your mind free of the enchanted table. Match your Mentality against the power of the table's spell (9). If you succeed, turn to **316**. If you fail, return to the beginning of this section.

296

'So it's you at last,' says the occupant of the room, a large man in an ill-fitting blue suit and pair of dark glasses. 'I've been expecting you. Colonel Hiram T. Schroeder, US Army retired, at your service.'

Perhaps Colonel Schroeder is blind and has mistaken you for an invited guest; certainly, you have never seen him before. You are about to apologise for your intrusion when he disconcertingly replies, 'No, not blind! I did expect you, or rather we both expected you. I suggest you take a seat and I'll explain.' Turn to **87**.

297

In one fluid movement you turn, block the maidservant's dagger arm, and push her backwards. Your opponent has a Stamina of 16 (note this on your Character Profile). How will you deal with this situation? Will you draw your pistol? Turn to **52**. Or will you try to wrest the dagger from her hand? Turn to **176**.

298

Desperately, you struggle to free yourself from the assassin-bug's embrace of death. Match your Strength against the creature's Strength (8) on the Conflict Table. If you fail, turn to **271**. If you succeed, will you use your pistol? Turn to **314**. Or, if your magazine is empty, will you engage in hand-to-hand combat? Turn to **352**.

299

You have lost 1 point of Endurance. The thing is enormous, but semi-translucent. Large baleful eyes stare at you and a mouth, which seems to divide the creature in two, drops open to reveal rows of sharp teeth. In the creature's sag-belly you can see the floating shadow of the dead Egyptian porter.

The toad-thing has a Stamina of 16 (note this on your Character Profile). Will you use your pistol? Turn to **332**. Or will you use one of the blazing fire-brands? Turn to **229**.

300

The hand tightens its grip about your throat! Roll against the thing's sorcerous Strength (8). If it succeeds, a further 2 points of Stamina are squeezed from your body. If you are reduced to zero, turn to **254**.

Desperately, you try to prise loose the skeletal talons. Match your Strength against the Hand of Glory's Strength on the Conflict Table. If you succeed, turn to **273**. If you fail, the beast tightens its grip. Return and repeat the first paragraph of this section.

301

Shaking your head, you pull the brain out of the jar and squeeze it. Ausbach screams and staggers back to the altar. His legs buckle and he falls to his knees. You squeeze again and he clutches his head, swaying from side to side, then he crumples to the ground. Where the brain was, dust now fills your hand; where Ausbach died, there are only his clothes and a faint brown outline.

A hissing draws your eyes back to the pillar of fire. Emerging from a nebulous haze at the centre of the fire is a monstrous snake head!

You must act swiftly to close the gateway Ausbach has opened. Your only hope is to destroy the pyramidion. Will

you use Thoth's mace? Turn to **342**. The khephera sword, the knobkerrie or the swordstick? Turn to **355**. The dragon whistle? Turn to **319**. Or will you snatch the pyramidion from the altar and hurl it into the pit? Turn to **224**.

302

Fishing the coin from your pocket, you drop it into the ferryman's hand and jump upon the soggy earth of the underworld.

'I thank you, mortal,' calls the ferryman. 'The one you seek lies yonder at the pit of time, yet you may learn wisdom at the halls of the dead.'

How will you react to this strange advice? Will you head towards a ruined temple-like building to your left? Turn to **364**. Or will you strike out in the direction the ferryman points, straight towards Ausbach? Turn to **337**.

303

As you concentrate, you realise the cap can be used to channel your thoughts against other intelligent creatures. You decide to try and force the ka away. Match your Mentality against the ka's Mentality of 5 on the Conflict Table. If you succeed, turn to **331**. If you fail, turn to **311**.

304

The door opens to reveal a library. Two windows and a pair of oak doors in the east wall are the only features which provide relief from the rows of leather-bound books, reports and files. Below the west window stands a desk, covered with papers and the model of an Egyptian pyramid. Without hesitation, you step forward to examine the desk. Turn to **284**.

305

Gritting your teeth, you lift the pyramidion and hurl it into the pit. For a second it flashes in the flames, then it plummets out of sight and the pillar of fire roars with fury. Shielding your face, you back away. You look up to see the giant outline of Het, with the flames writhing around her. She reaches out a huge taloned hand to seize you, then the flames falter and she tumbles back into the pit. You have closed the gateway!

As you turn to leave, the ground shudders beneath you, great cracks open at your feet and a biting wind howls out of the sky. Panicking, you leap the rift in the earth and run for the edge of the stone circle. Before you can reach it, the wind tears your feet from the ground and sends you spinning up into the sky. A chill fills your body as you watch the land slip away and the pit become a faint dot. Then the wind fails, you begin to fall and everything goes black. Turn to **375**.

306

The villagers' curiosity quickly overcomes their natural reticence and the two at the bar begin to chat with you. Deftly you steer the conversation away from yourself and on to the subject of Shandwick House, questioning them about its owner.

They tell you it is a large building occupied by Sir Roderick and his son Harold, who are both famous archaeologists. Harold is abroad at the moment but Sir Roderick is at home and has recently been entertaining a foreign baron who left only this morning. Finally, the villagers start to tell you about Sir Roderick's collection of old pots and statues which he keeps in a special room on the first floor of the house.

Armed with this information, you decide to take your leave, so you finish your drink and say goodbye, noticing only then that the gamekeeper is no longer in the bar. Buttoning up your coat, you step outside and climb into the car. Turn to **274**.

307

Once again, the power of the storm returns. The figure at the rail turns and you shudder as you recognise the cruel features of the corpse-man from the British Museum.

Ausbach lifts on high both hands and screams, 'Let the power of Wendigo, walker on wind, flow through my body.'

As if in answer, the wind howls and shrieks. Thunder peals and a bolt of lightning stabs into his body. The corpse-man shudders, yet remains standing. His eyes begin to glow an inhuman blue and a flickering skein of electricity shrouds his body. Roll against your Mentality. If you succeed, turn to **263**. If you fail, turn to **243**.

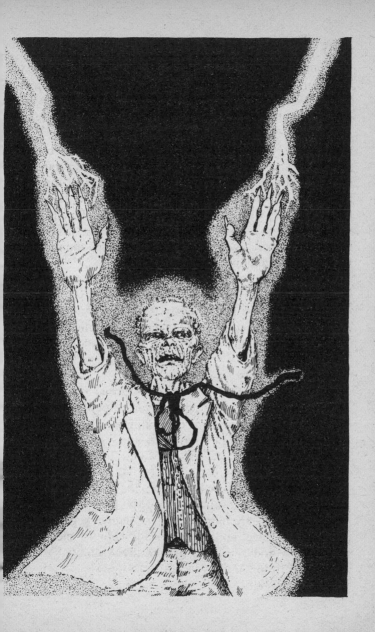

308

The plane climbs into the dark night sky. Your existence is reduced to the area illuminated by the pale reading light. For a while you read a newspaper, but the cold chills your bones. So you abandon the paper and try to sleep on an improvised bed of musty mail bags. Time passes and you doze.

You are roused by a series of inexplicable and alarming noises emitted through the voice tube: strange hissings and clickings, followed by a stifled shout from the pilot.

'Mein Gott . . .' Then silence.

Will you try to hail the pilot over the voice tube? Turn to **282**. Or will you make your way forward to the cabin and investigate? Turn to **246**.

309

As you and Harold retreat towards an archway, a gang of the loathsome bogies attack. Roll four dice and note the total on your Character Profile. This figure represents the total Stamina of all the bogies in the gang and you must reduce it to zero to kill all the bogies.

Quickly, you grab a corpse dust pot and hurl it at the creatures (cross it off your Character Profile). Roll against your Dexterity. If you succeed, the pot bursts, inflicting the roll of three six-sided dice on the bogies' Stamina. If all the bogies are slain, turn to **106**.

If any of the creatures survive, or if you missed, they press home their attack. Roll against their Dexterity of 9. If they are successful, their teeth and malformed hands tear 3 points from your Stamina. If your Stamina is reduced to zero, turn to **63**. If not, you can try to escape with Harold through the archway door. Turn to **268**. Or you can cast another corpse dust pot by returning to the second paragraph of this section.

Desperately, you run forward shouting, 'Stop! The game is up!'

The man flings out his left arm and a shower of glistening golden particles arches through the air towards another display cabinet. A moment later you are upon the thief and grab him by the shoulder. You wrench him round to face you and gasp at his hellish visage. His skin is stretched taut over his skull, his lips are curled back in a dreadful leer, showing a mouth too full of teeth, and his red-rimmed eyes have an evil gleam. Then the corpse-man pulls free of your grip, plunges into the sarcophagus and disappears!

Roll against your Mentality. Whether you succeed or fail, turn to **227**.

As you try to force the ka back, you lose control. Another force, which seems to gloat over you, pours into your mind. A tremendous feeling of vertigo overwhelms you and you fall to the dust. Slowly, your life begins to drain away, a chill fills your body and you slip into torment.

The cap was an artefact dedicated to the monstrous deity, Yehog. In failing to control it, he was able to consume your mind. This is the end of the adventure for you.

With a yell of defiance, you fling yourself at the hunchback, grab his upraised cleaver arm and thrust him back against a dresser. China cascades across the tiled floor as you both struggle for supremacy. Can you disarm the hunchback or will he break your hold and strike you with the cleaver? Match your Strength against the hunchback's Strength (9) on the Conflict Table. If you succeed, turn to **85**. If you fail, turn to **13**.

313

On the right of the corridor light pours out of a doorway, before which a circle has been drawn on the ground. Inside the circle, the stubs of candles still smoulder and there are puddles of different coloured oils; you have discovered the remnants of the preparations Ausbach mixed to open the gateway to the underworld.

Creeping forward, you peer round the edge of the doorway into a chamber lit by oil lamps. The chamber is empty but its walls are decorated with elaborate representations of the Egyptian gods. Set into the wall opposite you is a gilded door and beside this is a representation of Thoth, sitting at a high desk.

Stepping into the chamber, you admire the picture and

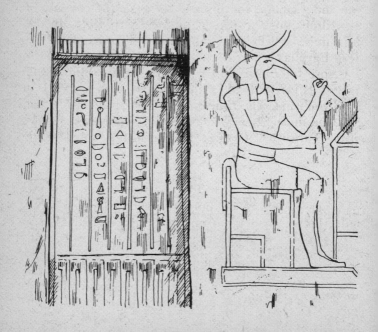

the god's head turns to stare at you with dark eyes! If you have any ammunition, you may fire up to three times. Turn to **123**. If you do not wish to fire, or cannot, turn to **150**.

314

The creature scuttles back to the pilot's corpse and prepares to spring at you from this perch. Quickly, you bring the pistol to bear and open fire. You may fire one, two or three bullets as you wish, remembering to roll against your Dexterity for accuracy. Total the damage caused and deduct the number of bullets fired from your Character Profile. Whatever happens, turn to **339**.

315

You have lost 2 points of Endurance. The thing is enormous, but semi-translucent. Large baleful eyes regard you and a mouth, which seems to divide the creature in two, drops open to reveal rows of sharp teeth. In the creature's sag-belly you can see the floating shadow of the dead Egyptian porter.

Before you can react, the creature darts forward. Roll against its Dexterity of 8. If it succeeds, turn to **267**. If it fails, you leap away. Note on your Character Profile that the toad-thing has a Stamina of 16. Will you use your pistol? Turn to **332**. Or one of the blazing fire-brands? Turn to **229**.

316

With a gasp, you wrench yourself free of the Dragon Table and its hideous spell is broken. Shivering, you beat a hasty retreat from the diabolical room and slam the door. Back in the corridor you massage life back into your numb hands and recover 1 point of Endurance.

Will you now continue north along the corridor? Turn to **172**. Or will you try the door opposite in the east wall? Turn to **138**.

317

The maidservant's dagger pierces your chest. You gasp, your knees buckle and you topple to the floor. The woman kneels beside you and whispers to you in a strange hissing voice.

'My master will be pleased. At last he is rid of his only human foe.' This adventure is at an end for you.

318

You fall heavily and your ankle cracks. Howling with pain, you collapse in a writhing heap. Ausbach leaps forward and casts a black ball at you. The object smashes on the flagstones and erupts in a cloud of smoking, choking, black dust.

'From dust you came and to dust you shall return,' he screams. Your body withers, slumps to the ground and crumbles into dust. Thus ends your adventure.

Pulling out the whistle, you begin to blow on it in the hope that the sound may shatter the crystal. But the pyramidion just glows brighter and a horrible warbling fills the air. Alarmed, you lower the whistle, but the sound grows stronger and is joined by the heavy flap of wings. The whistle commands a beast of the Outer Darkness related to the Wind God, Wendigo. Normally, the summoner is separated from the beast by the dimensions which bind it to its own world and it can only affect the areas or things the summoner desires. But, because of Ausbach's gateway, the monster has been able to break through and now it is hunting for its tormentor – you!

Turning, you flee from the altar, fumbling for a weapon. Out of the flames behind you flaps a vast bulbous beast. Its wings of stretched membrane and bone are attached to the length of its body and its mouth is bordered by fleshy lips which whistle as it chases you. This is the end of the adventure for you.

As you explore the north side of the house, you stumble across what must have been the scullery and tradesmen's entrance. On tiptoe you approach the door and test the handle. To your surprise, the door is unlocked and swings inward on well-oiled hinges, to reveal a large kitchen area. The room is dimly lit by the guttering stumps of two candles, which sprout from ornate candleholders, and the dying embers of a log fire. You enter the kitchen and latch the door behind you, then move towards a large table which stands in the middle of the room. It bears the candleholders and a half-eaten plate of stew. As you wait for your eyes to adjust to the gloom, you hear the soft tread of someone close behind you. Roll against your Dexterity. If you succeed, turn to **345**. If you fail, turn to **366**.

321

You close the book and look up at Colonel Schroeder. 'I am sure,' he says, 'that what you have read will have raised more questions than it furnished answers. My little book contains much which is unintelligible for you at present.'

You return the book and, as he takes it back, the Colonel says, 'Finally, I have a small gift.' He passes you a glass tube which contains lurid mauve crystals. 'They can provide a most potent restorative. In extremis, you can survive by imbibing the entire contents of the phial.'

If you wish to accept the phial, enter it on your Character Profile as Mauve Crystals **285**. At any time hereafter, you can choose to swallow the crystals. When you do, turn to entry **285** and follow the instructions. Remember to take note of your current entry though!

'Now you must leave me,' the Colonel continues, 'for I am very tired. Yet before you go, I must give you two warnings. The first is, beware of Ausbach. He is a servitor of Het the Destroyer and plots the downfall of all mankind. Second, I have given you the knowledge of means to obtain forbidden lore; use it well. Use it badly and you will become tainted by the chaos which is the Outer Darkness. Look on me and beware!'

Colonel Hiram T. Schroeder rises and tugs the dark

glasses from his face. You stare into a pair of huge bulging snake eyes! Roll against your Mentality. If you succeed, turn to **244**. If you fail, turn to **265**.

322

Ausbach's spell grips your mind. Your hands grow numb and you drop the jar. He chuckles and, pointing towards you, he utters a horrible clicking sound. Immediately a fiery hand sprouts from the pillar of fire and arches towards you!

Will you dive towards Ausbach? Turn to **330**. Or will you dive for the jar? Turn to **293**.

323

The engines scream to fever pitch and the plane's fuselage begins to vibrate. Suddenly, you are through the clouds and falling towards a crazily spinning wall of white: the ground! This is the end of the adventure for you.

324

Unable to take the pain, you drop the pyramidion and a horrible laughter fills the sky. Looking up, you see Het stepping out of the pillar of fire and, where her feet tread, smoke rises. A greedy hand sweeps down towards you. As you turn to run, it clutches you in a burning embrace. You have failed to close the gateway. This is the end of the adventure for you.

325

The doors swing back to reveal a large display room, filled with exhibits from ancient Egypt. Figurines of the gods, talismans, jewellery and carefully preserved hieroglyphic texts line the walls, whilst the floor is covered with statues, amphori and other relics from the Pharaohs. But the centre of the room has been cleared for the up-ended bottom of a sarcophagus. Nearby lies the discarded lid, its gold embellishments glowing in the light from your torch.

You have found the other end of the Thaati Gateway the thief used to escape from the British Museum. Perhaps the pyramidion is somewhere in this room? Searching wildly, you can discover nothing which even remotely resembles the stolen artefact, but you do find a heavy oak door set back into the north wall of the room.

Will you open this door? Turn to **304**. Or will you return to the landing to explore the south hallway? Turn to **204**. Or the north hallway? Turn to **245**.

Raising your weapon, you lash out at the ka. Roll against your Dexterity. If you succeed, deduct your weapon's damage from the ka's Stamina (or, if you are using Thoth's mace, its Endurance). If you reduce the creature's rating to zero, turn to **367**.

If the ka survives, it will attack you. Roll against its Dexterity of 8. If it succeeds, its talons will slash your body, causing 2 points of Stamina damage. If this reduces your rating to zero, turn to **228**.

If you survive, you may continue the battle by returning to the first paragraph of this section. Otherwise, if you have any ammunition, you may draw your pistol. Turn to **347**.

327

The descent is long and gruelling and your muscles ache horribly. But, eventually, your feet touch the cavern's floor. Striking a match, you relight the lantern to view your surroundings. Turn to **374**.

328

The ladder rungs are occasionally illuminated by brief stabs of lightning as you climb up towards your encounter with a twentieth-century wizard. You emerge atop the *Lucretia* and struggle out into a rainswept howling wind. A wooden walkway, bounded on either side by a metal handrail, leads away forward. To either side, the corrugated back of the airship falls away towards the depths of the sky. Up ahead, silhouetted against the thunderclouds, stands your adversary. You grip the handrail and push your body into the wind.

You halt a few yards from the man. The roar of the storm suddenly fades, yet the clouds still scud across the sky and the lightning flickers. A cruel thin voice, tinged with a Germanic accent, speaks to you.

'In Wales you spoiled my plans and robbed me of my prize. The pyramidion you claimed as a souvenir is a key which will unlock the hideous power of my mistress, Het the Destroyer. She shall wreak destruction upon mankind and I, Ausbach, shall rule the living dead after her. Only you and that bumbling fool, Charles Petrie-Smith, have stood against me. Now you will perish.' Turn to **307**.

329

You hand over the artefact.

The ferryman weighs it in his hands, then returns it, saying, 'I have no use for this, mortal. Give me, instead, a piece of your life-force.' With these words he passes his bony hand into your chest! You gasp and feel a chill pain.

Then the hand is removed. You have lost 1 point of Endurance. If you survive, the ferryman speaks again.

'The one you seek lies yonder at the pit of time.'

The creature points away across the grey landscape, towards a squat clump of black trees. Yet you can also see, away to your left, a ruined temple-like building. Will you make your way towards the pit of time and Ausbach? Turn to **337**. Or will you explore the temple? Turn to **364**.

330

Your action catches Ausbach by surprise. He stands stock-still as you dive to the ground in front of him. The fiery hand flames over you. It singes your clothes and engulfs the Baron. His screams fill the air as he is swept up to the pillar of fire; then all you can hear is the roar of the flames. Het has claimed her own.

Shaking, you rise to your feet. A nebulous haze is writhing at the pillar's centre, from which a monstrous snake head is beginning to emerge! You must act swiftly to reverse Ausbach's spell. Your only hope is to destroy the pyramidion.

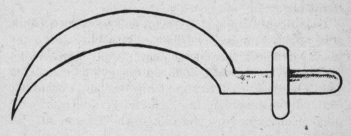

Will you use Thoth's mace? Turn to **342**. The khephera sword, knobkerrie or swordstick? Turn to **355**. The dragon whistle? Turn to **319**. Or will you snatch the pyramidion from the altar and hurl it into the pit? Turn to **224**.

331

You will the ka to retreat and it hesitates, flapping around you without driving home its attack. Redoubling your efforts, you hurl your will at the creature. Another will overrides your thoughts. With an inhuman cry, the ka collapses to the ground. It screams again in agony and then its head crumples like a paper bag.

Horrified, you lose 2 points of Endurance. You stagger away, tearing the crocodile cap from your head. You feel a pulsing in your mind and know instinctively that you have just been used by the forces of the Outer Darkness to destroy a life. Skirting the ka's body, you trudge on along the track which now rises steeply up the side of a broad slope. Turn to **289**.

332

Realising you should keep some distance between yourself and the toad-thing, you back away. Suddenly a gun explodes behind you and you bump into Petrie-Smith.

'There's another one!' he exclaims. 'You must deal with this fellow.'

You draw your pistol. At this range you can hardly miss, but what effect will the weapon have? You may fire one, two or three bullets. Roll each time against your Dexterity, for accuracy. Calculate the damage you have caused, deduct the bullets fired from your Character Profile, then turn to **351**.

333

You have entered a reception room, whose walls are lined with glass display cases. The torch beam flashes over a collection of objects which seem to be curios from the East: here a procession of ivory and jade Buddhas, there a grotesque group of bronze Hindu deities. Other cases present a collection of musical instruments: pipes, horns and curious drums. However, pride of place has been given to a gold and glass box which houses a whistle, carved from ivory, in the form of a roaring writhing dragon. A presentation card declares: 'Dragon whistle. Carved by Tibetan cultists c. 15th Century AD. Considered to be a magic weapon.'

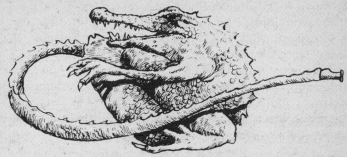

You have heard, from Petrie-Smith, curious stories of such artefacts. If you wish to take the whistle, note it on your Character Profile under Possessions. An open door leads from the room, turn to **356**.

334

You rush down the stairs two at a time, shouting at the top of your voice. Ausbach wavers before his infernal machine as you run across the hall towards him. Then suddenly he grabs the table, which is on castors, and propels his victim towards you. The table sends you crashing to the flagstones and you suffer a 1 point loss to your Stamina.

Ausbach takes advantage of your discomfort to flee from the hall, shouting, 'I have more important matters to attend to than your destruction. I leave you both to my pets!'

You fumble with the leather thongs which bind the young man to the table. Weakly, he struggles upright and introduces himself as Harold Lathers.

'I fear that we can expect no mercy from Ausbach's pets,' he says. 'See, they come! These are the results of Ausbach's vile experiments: the living dead and the never-to-be-born. They thirst for our blood and slaver for our life-force!'

Into the hall hops, staggers and crawls a pack of jibbering bogies. Some cavort on stunted bird-like legs, others pull unspeakable serpent-like bodies along the flagstones. They smack their thin decayed lips and an evil expectant gleam lights their eyes.

Roll against your Mentality. If you succeed, turn to **358**. If you fail, turn to **373**.

335

You sweep a candleholder from the table, scattering molten wax across the room. The hunchback sniggers and a malicious grin spreads over his ugly face. Who will strike the next blow in this nocturnal battle? Match your Dexterity against the hunchback's Dexterity (6) on the Conflict Table. If you succeed, turn to **247**. If you fail, turn to **143**.

336

Colonel Schroeder reaches inside his jacket and draws out a small leatherbound book.

'You have pursued Ausbach because he stole something from you. Your pyramidion is the key to terrible power. It is time to learn the nature of that power. Time to step beyond the forbidden gateway that shields mankind from the terrors of the Outer Darkness. Turn to page twelve of my little book and read what you find there.' Turn to **354**.

*337

The track to the pit of time leads across a barren plain, towards a clump of gnarled and stunted trees. As you pass beneath their dark branches, a curious wittering disturbs the still air. With a whirr of wings, a bird-like creature settles a few yards in front of you. You have encountered a ka, a spirit lost in the underworld.

The ka's body is similar in size to your own, but it is covered with dusty grey feathers and a pair of wings, now folded on its back, sprout from its shoulders. The ka's head is bald, like a vulture's. Two sharp red eyes glare over a curved beak, regarding you intently.

The ka has a Stamina of 12 and an Endurance of 10 (note this on your Character Profile). Now roll against your Mentality. If you succeed, turn to **167**. If you fail, turn to **189**.

338

You reach your cabin, open the door, then flop upon the reassuringly soft bed. Every joint in your body throbs and your head feels numb. A great weariness seeps through your being. Gradually, you slip into a fitful slumber, disturbed by the endless churning of words and images from the past few days.

You awake with a start, lying on your side facing the cabin door. A yellowish mist is invading the cabin! Your nose feels dry and a salty taste haunts your mouth. Sulphur! Desperately, you try to rise but your body seems paralysed. Now the mist begins to glow and a strange humming sound fills your ears. Crude red letters begin to glow before your eyes.

'I, Ausbach, tire of your meddling. Come to me atop the airship, or perish here in your bed.'

The words hang in the air for a few moments, then begin to fade. Twilight's gloom seeps back into the cabin as the mist dissolves. It is as if the strange display never was, yet a smell of sulphur lingers on. Strength returns to your limbs and you rise. Your bedside clock shows the time to be half-past six. You must have been asleep for several hours, yet you have recovered no Stamina or Endurance.

If you have the serpent glass, you could make use of it. Turn to **365**. Otherwise, gather your possessions, reload your pistol, then leave the cabin. Turn to **349**.

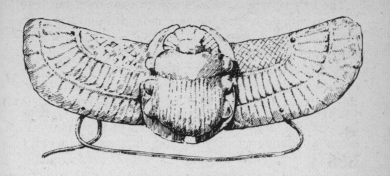

339

If your gunfire has reduced the assassin-bug's Stamina to
zero, turn to **230**. If the creature still lives, it will attack you
again. Roll against its Dexterity of 8. If it succeeds, turn to
259. If it fails, will you fight on with your pistol, presuming
you have some bullets left? Turn to **314**. Or will you engage
the creature in hand-to-hand combat? Turn to **352**.

340

The descent is longer than you expected. Your muscles
begin to ache and your arms and legs shake uncontrollably
under the strain. Then your left arm slips and you are
plummeting through the darkness!

The fall is short and your landing is cushioned by
something that shatters beneath you. Lose 2 points of
Stamina. Crawling from the wreckage, you strike a match
and, in its fitful glare, examine the object that has saved
you. It is a giant clay model of a crab! The shell has been
crushed by your fall and the legs lie scattered across the
ground. The match expires, plunging you into darkness.
Fumbling for the lantern, which is battered but still
usable, you light its wick and survey your new
surroundings. Turn to **374**.

341

The creature's sharp teeth clamp round your body, then it gulps. In one swift movement, you are propelled into the creature's sag-belly. This adventure is at an end for you.

342

Glowing with a luminous blue light, the pyramidion lies on the altar. Rushing forward, you raise the mace and swing it down, shattering the crystal and releasing its pent-up energies in a burst of sound and light. Momentarily blinded, you stagger back and a nerve-grating screech

bursts from the air overhead. Blinking, you look up to see the giant outline of Het writhing in the flames. She reaches out with a huge taloned hand to grasp you, then the flames falter and she tumbles back into the pit with a howl of fury. You have closed the gateway!

But, as you turn to leave, the ground shudders beneath you, great cracks open at your feet and a biting wind howls out of the sky. Panicking, you leap the rift in the earth and run for the edge of the stone circle. Before you can reach it, the wind tears your feet from the ground and sends you spinning up into the sky. A chill fills your body as you watch the land slip away and the pit become a faint dot. Then the wind fails, you begin to fall and everything goes black. Turn to **375**.

343

On the landing you find an imposing set of double doors, set between two busts of nineteenth-century generals. Hallways lead off the landing to the north and south. Will you open the double doors? Turn to **325**. Take the north hallway? Turn to **245**. Or take the south hallway? Turn to **204**.

344

You tug sharply and hurl Ausbach over your head. With a terrible scream, he plummets into the flames below and disappears from sight. You have destroyed Ausbach at last!

A hissing draws your eyes back to the pillar of fire. Emerging from a nebulous haze that writhes at its centre is a hideous snake head! You must act swiftly to close the gateway Ausbach has opened. Your only hope is to destroy the pyramidion. But how?

Will you use Thoth's mace? Turn to **342**. The khephera sword, knobkerrie or swordstick? Turn to **355**. The dragon whistle? Turn to **319**. Or will you snatch the pyramidion from the altar and cast it into the pit after Ausbach's flaming corpse? Turn to **224**.

345

You spin around just in time to confront a figure armed with a meat cleaver! Desperately, you side-step your attacker and the cleaver slashes the air where you stood.

Your attacker is a shuffling haggard hunchback. His skin is grey and pockmarked like one who has been disinterred from the grave. His clothes hang in tatters and his breath is foul. As he lifts the cleaver for another blow, you have no time to draw your pistol. Will you try instead to grab one of the heavy candleholders from the table? Turn to **335**. Or will you charge the hunchback and wrest the cleaver from his grip? Turn to **312**.

346

Together, you rush towards the shelf. Some of the bogies surge at you. Their leader, a thing like a giant hedgehog, grabs for your shoulder, but you thrust it aside and reach your goal.

'Here!' cries Harold. 'These clay pots contain something Ausbach calls corpse dust. He flings it at the creatures and they crumble away into dust. Come, we must make for that archway and escape from this accursed laboratory.'

There are three corpse dust pots in the box. Note them on your Character Profile as 3 Corpse Dust Pots 3D6/–. When you throw one of the pots, roll against your Dexterity. If you are successful, the pot bursts, releasing a cloud of poisonous dust. This inflicts damage to the creatures' Stamina equivalent to the roll of three dice (3D6). If you fail your Dexterity roll, the pot does not burst. Now turn to **309**.

347

You draw the pistol and squeeze the trigger. You may fire one, two or three bullets at the ka. However, the ka is not an easy target. Its grey feathers blur its outline in the

twilight and the beat of its wings over your head is confusing. To hit, you must subtract one from your Dexterity and then roll under the modified score. If you hit and kill the ka, turn to **367**.

If the ka survives, it will attack you. Roll against its Dexterity (8). If it succeeds, its talons will slash your body, inflicting 2 points of Stamina damage. If this reduces your rating to zero, turn to **228**.

If you survive, you may continue the battle by returning to the first paragraph of this section. Otherwise, you may draw the khephera sword. Turn to **249**. Or arm yourself with Thoth's mace, the knobkerrie or the swordstick. Turn to **326**.

In one easy motion, you leap from the boat into the sucking mud below. Struggling to free your feet, you see the ferryman dissolve and then rematerialise beside you. Once more he stretches out his bony hand, but this time it plunges into your chest! A chill grip tightens around your heart and the ferryman whispers in your ear.

'Foolish mortal! Now I will carry you to the realm of the dead in a very different way!'

With a groan, you crumple to the ground. The ferryman lifts your body, to return it to the wharf. This is the end of your adventure.

You slip out into the deserted corridor. In the distance you can hear the murmur of conversation and the clatter of pans; your fellow passengers are at dinner. You, however, turn away from their inviting clamour and head towards the airship's dark unheated hold.

You slip through a door marked Crew Only and enter an enormous space, criss-crossed by glimmering metal walkways and stuffed with enormous, waxed-canvas, gas bags. For a moment you pause. The warmth of the airship's living quarters gradually flows from your body, the darkness enfolds you. What horror, beyond reason, waits for you atop the *Lucretia*?

As you traverse the airship's walkways, you pass a variety of valves and dials which must, presumably, control the gas bags and ballast. Once, you are obliged to hide from a maintenance crew, but at last you reach the base of a ladder, which must surely lead out on to the top of the airship. Now above the roar of the airship's engines you can hear the howling fury of a storm. Turn to **328**.

350

The mail plane, a gleaming, three-engined, Junkers monoplane, is packed with mail bags and freight. You are the only passenger. The pilot, a friendly Viennese, shows you to your makeshift seat.

'The flight will be a little chilly,' he warns, and hands you some blankets. 'We fly east along the Alps, over Innsbruck, Salzburg and Lintz. Then we turn north-east for Vienna. We arrive before dawn.' He moves forward to his cabin and shuts the door.

You settle into your uncomfortable accommodation, while the pilot powers up the plane's engines. To your left is a window. In front is a bulkhead, which supports a voice tube, shelf and reading light. The pilot hails you down the voice tube.

'Be prepared. We take off now.' The engines roar into life and the plane rolls forward.

As the Junkers taxis towards the take-off point, you wipe the condensation from the window and peer out. In the glare of an illuminated hangar you see a black limousine slide to a halt. A curiously hunched figure emerges from the car and, as the character disappears from view, you gain the distinct impression that he was waving you goodbye. Turn to **308**.

351

If your gunfire has reduced the toad-thing's Stamina to zero, turn to **288**. If not, it lumbers forward to attack.

Roll against the toad-thing's Dexterity (8). If it succeeds, turn to **267**. If it fails, the sag-belly thumps into you. Can you keep your balance? Match the creature's Strength (8) against your own Strength on the Conflict Table. If it succeeds, turn to **368**. It if fails, how will you counter-attack? With the fire-brand? Turn to **229**. Or will you fire again?

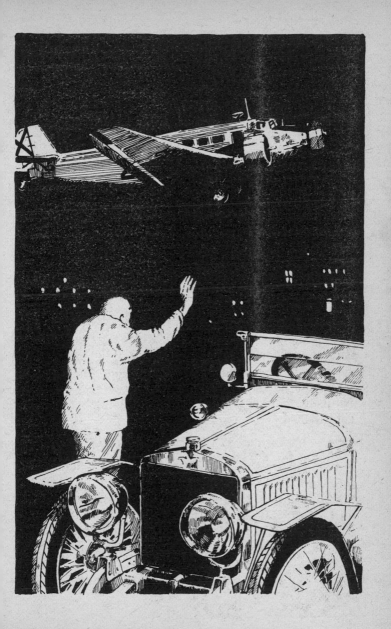

If this is your choice, you may fire one, two or three bullets. Roll against your Dexterity each time you fire, to check accuracy. Total the damage you have caused, deduct the bullets fired from your Character Profile, then return to the start of this section.

352

Now the combat becomes a deadly hand and claw struggle. You are armed with an improvised weapon: your gun butt, or the empty fire extinguisher.

You attack first. Roll against your Dexterity. If you succeed, crush 2 points from the creature's Stamina. If the creature is slain, turn to **230**. If it still lives, read on.

Now the assassin-bug attempts to sink its poisoned fangs into your body. Roll against the creature's Dexterity (8). If it succeeds, you suffer the loss of 2 points of Stamina. If you are reduced to zero, turn to **271**. If not, you continue the battle. Return and repeat the second paragraph of this section.

353

The wheezing, creaking corpse-thing seems intent upon ensnaring you. It probes the air in front with clumsy sweeps

of its scrawny bandaged arms. You take a step backwards and your feet crunch on broken glass. The mummy halts, cocks its head as if listening, then turns to face you.

Boldly, you stand your ground, then dodge the creature's first ill-timed attempt to grab you. Now you can attempt to skewer the thing. Roll against your Dexterity. If you succeed, deduct the damage from the mummy's Stamina (6). If your attack is successful, turn to **363**. If you failed, turn to **147**.

354

This is what you find on page twelve of the book:

'Before time itself, there was nothing except the chaos of the Outer Darkness, an awesome intelligence. When the universe we inhabit was created, this primordial entity was split asunder and flung throughout the cosmos. It dwells here still. I learnt its names from the gruesome mythology of the Egyptians. Studied its nature in the clay Sanskrit tablets of India's ancient cities. While, in the bas-reliefs at the forbidden Mayan temple of Chuqua, I saw its hideous power.

'In all, I have discovered five manifestations of the Outer Darkness. First, there is Het the Destroyer; her element is fire, her guise the snake. Second, is Yehog, the devourer within; his element is spirit and his guise a hog. Then there is Wendigo, walker on the wind; Byelbog, who broods beneath the sea; and Apep, who walks restlessly through the earth.

'These five terrors forever lurk behind the everyday. Yet there are also mysterious and beneficent entities who set protective rings about man's puny consciousness. Chief among these Keepers is one who was known to the Egyptians as Thoth. He combines all five elements of the Outer Darkness, tempered with the power of knowledge. The Keepers appear to be patrons to all sentient beings, for in them can be found, in harmony, all six elements.' Turn to **321**.

355

Glowing with a luminous blue light, the pyramidion lies on the altar. Rushing forward, you raise your weapon and swing it down, shattering the crystal and releasing its pent-up energies in an explosion of light and sound. Your body shudders with the discharge and, momentarily blinded, you collapse on the ground. Lose 3 points of Stamina.

Looking up, you see the giant outline of Het writhing in the flames. She reaches out with a huge taloned hand to grasp you, but even as she moves, the fire falters and with a howl of fury she collapses back into the pit. You have closed the gateway!

But, even as you turn to leave, the ground shudders beneath you; great cracks open at your feet and a biting wind howls out of the sky. Panicking, you leap the rift in the earth and run for the edge of the stone circle. Before you can reach it, the wind tears your feet from the ground and sends you spinning up into the sky. A chill fills your body as you watch the land slip away and the pit become a faint dot. Then the wind fails, you begin to fall and everything goes black. Turn to **375**.

356

This seems to be the entrance hall of Shandwick House. A large, exquisitely carved staircase rises up the north wall to a balcony landing, which runs the whole length of the west wall. The furniture is, however, sparse. A coat stand (devoid of coats) is placed close to the foot of the stairs. Opposite, in the south-east corner of the hall, stands a suit of armour and a small round table. Several letters lie scattered across the table top.

Will you examine the letters? Turn to **370**. Or will you climb the stairs? Turn to **343**.

You miss the ka and it climbs into the air, circling over you and crying in its inhuman voice. Out of the gloom come two more of the creatures and all three dive upon you!

In this fight you will have the first blow. If you hit a ka, your khephera will inflict double its usual damage factor. To hit a ka, you must roll under your Dexterity and you may only make one such roll per combat round. The surviving kas will then attack you with their talons. Each one has a separate attack and must roll under its Dexterity (8) to hit you. If it is successful, it will inflict 2 points of Stamina damage. Each ka has a Stamina of 12 and Endurance of 10.

The combat will continue until either you or the kas triumph. If the kas win, they will feast on your body and the adventure ends here. If you succeed in killing the kas, you may proceed to the pit of time. Turn to **289**.

This vile repellent sight has cost you 1 point of Endurance. You and Harold stand in the middle of the great hall, while the creatures swarm over the machinery, seeking to surround you. How can you survive this horde? You will need some weapon suitable for mass combat.

Harold Lathers shouts, 'Quick! On that shelf is a weapon Ausbach uses upon those pets who displease him.'

Will you heed Harold's advice? Turn to **346**. Or will you grab one of the medieval weapons from the wall to your left? Turn to **148**.

You lose 1 point of Endurance as you gaze at this terror. This is no freak of nature, but a clay model animated by sorcery to defend Khefu's pyramid. The creature clatters forward to the attack. It has a Stamina of 12. Note this on your Character Profile.

How will you deal with the terracotta scorpion? Run away? Turn to **281**. Draw your pistol? Turn to **264**. Use your knobkerrie or your swordstick? Turn to **231**. Or pipe upon the dragon whistle? Turn to **200**.

360

At the last moment Ausbach tries to leap aside and you catch him awkwardly. He grabs your shoulders and, the next you know, you are rolling with him across the ground. You stop on the edge of the pit with the flames licking up around your head. Ausbach grins evilly down into your face.

You must try to topple him into the pit. Match your Strength against Ausbach's Strength (9) on the Conflict Table. If you succeed, turn to **344**. If you fail, turn to **286**.

361

As you cross the room, you notice movement by the fireplace. The chimney seems to be smoking. However, the torch beam reveals that smoke is pouring, not from the fireplace, but from the curious painting above the mantelpiece. Something horrid is forming out of a turmoil of oily black smoke. A scaly loathsome creature which is continually flickering into and out of substance. Roll against your Mentality. If you succeed, turn to **24**. If you fail, turn to **4**.

362

The engines whine and you feel your safety straps tighten. The aircraft has gone into a spin! As the blood thumps in your temples, you struggle to increase the plane's speed and pull it out of its death throes. Match your Dexterity against the plane's sluggish controls (9) on the Conflict Table. If you succeed, turn to **241**. If you fail, turn to **323**.

363

The sword point pierces the mummy's throat, grinds on bone and jams fast! The creature's vile whimpering becomes a horrid gurgling noise. Next the mummy begins to thrash about in an effort to dislodge the blade or tug the sword from your hand.

Match the mummy's sorcerous Strength (8) against your own Strength on the Conflict Table. If the creature succeeds, turn to **105**. If it fails, you wrench the blade free. Turn to **26**.

364

A thin mist rolls across the dusty track which leads towards the temple of the dead. The building is a ruin. Great columns have tumbled to the ground, bronze statues, headless and armless, rot beneath layers of verdigris. A thin plume of grey smoke escapes from the broken roof. Will you be bold and enter the temple? Turn to **56**. Or will you pick your way across the barren country to the pit of time? Turn to **337**.

365

Lose 1 Endurance point as you gaze in the serpent glass.

Mysterious shadows resolve into a vision across the broad back of the *Lucretia*. It is dark and a great storm is blowing. Great clouds rush past the airship and brief flashes of lightning cut through the gloom. The silhouette of a man stands atop the *Lucretia*, arms upraised. Suddenly, a bolt of lightning stabs into him. He shudders, yet remains standing. Now he turns towards you and flings one arm out in front of him. A dazzling coil of electricity arcs towards you, dispelling the vision in the serpent glass.

Clearly, this Ausbach is able to work potent magic. Your pistol may be more reassuring than effective. Now gather your possessions and leave the cabin. Turn to **349**.

366

Before you can react, you receive a stunning blow to your back which sends you reeling across the table. You have lost 3 points of Stamina. Gasping with pain, you turn to face your attacker: a shuffling haggard hunchback. His skin is grey and pockmarked like one who has been disinterred from the grave. His clothes hang in tatters and his breath is foul. As he raises a bloody meat cleaver for another blow, you have no time to draw your pistol. Will you try instead to grab one of the heavy candleholders from the table? Turn to **335**. Or will you charge the hunchback and wrest the cleaver from his grip? Turn to **312**.

367

An agonised scream escapes the ka's throat. Blood and feathers tumble out of the air and the bird-creature collapses at your feet. Turning its body with your toe, you see it is dead. Squaring your shoulders, you walk away towards the pit of time. Turn to **289**.

368

The fire-brand is knocked from your hand and you are sent sprawling backwards on the sand. Your only hope is to blast the creature before it can engulf you. If your pistol is empty, turn to **341**.

You may fire one, two or three bullets. Roll against your Dexterity each time for accuracy. Calculate the damage you have caused and deduct the bullets fired from your Character Profile. If you have finally slain the creature, turn to **288**. If it still lives, turn to **267**.

369

You awake in the morning having regained half of any Stamina or Endurance lost in last night's encounters. The butler has already reloaded your pistol and packed your bags. However, you take the precaution of adding a second magazine and either the knobkerrie or your swordstick to the baggage.

Descending to the study, you eat a hearty breakfast (recover 1 point of Stamina), while Petrie-Smith arranges his passage to Cairo and books a suite at the Grand Hotel. Breakfast over, the sage old man hands you an exquisitely carved scarab beetle on a leather thong. It seems to be made of an unusual blue crystal.

'This is a "Toofah" beetle,' he informs you. 'It is said Egyptian sorcerers used such artefacts to reflect the spells of their enemies. Of course, I have only read stories of such powers. However, if this Ausbach fellow is delving into the Outer Darkness, the blue scarab may be of use to you.

'I must confess,' he continues, winking at you, 'I am a robber. I "borrowed" the scarab from a curator friend yesterday. I do hope he won't miss it!' You thank Petrie-Smith for the gift, gather your bags together and leave the house. Enter the blue scarab on your Character Profile.

At the aerodrome, your club biplane has already been dragged from the hangar and powered up. Clambering in, you taxi downwind, open the throttle and roar into the sky. Unfortunately, the plane is infuriatingly slow and draughty. You endure a miserable flight to Paris, only to find the airship *Lucretia* has already left for Vienna. Your only hope of overtaking her now is to cadge a lift on the overnight mail plane. Turn to **350**.

Many of the letters, which are addressed to Sir Roderick Lathers, remain unopened. Yet, in addition, there are two envelopes addressed to a Baron Ausbach, c/o Shandwick House. The contents of the first envelope are missing, but from the postmark, you discern the letter was posted from Croydon aerodrome three days ago. The other envelope contains a letter from a person called Hiram T. Schroeder, who is advertised, on his letter heading, as 'A collector of curios and unusual anthropological specimens'. He has written to Baron Ausbach, to confirm a meeting between them at 3 pm on the 25th – in other words, earlier today! However, there is no mention of where the meeting took place. Replacing the envelopes on the table, you thoughtfully climb the stairs. Turn to **343**.

You engage the Purser in a conversation about the romance of airship flight. This seems to be a topic of some interest to the man, who begins to tell you anecdotes about passengers he has known. Soon you are able to guide him on to his thoughts about Baron Bachaus and Hiram T. Schroeder.

'A strange pair, those two,' observes the Purser. 'They boarded on the same ticket. The Baron keeps strictly to his cabin, attended only by his beautiful, but mute, maidservant or nurse. He appears to be an invalid of some kind. As for the American, well, he seems to be more gregarious. I've seen him in the bar once or twice. He's an explorer of some kind. Most of the time though he keeps to his cabin, with the curtains drawn . . .'

Once started, the Purser is difficult to stop, but believing you have obtained as much information as the man possesses, you make a suitable excuse and leave his office. Who will you investigate first? Baron Ausbach, in cabin 3?

Turn to **192**. Or the reclusive American, Hiram T. Schroeder, in cabin 7? Turn to **78**.

372

You ease yourself into the co-pilot's seat and grab the steering column. The plane is now in a shallow dive through a bank of thick cloud. Somewhere below lurk the jagged peaks of the Alps! Can you regain control of the plane before it falls into a spin or crashes into the mountains? Match your Dexterity against the plane's controls (7) on the Conflict Table. If you succeed, turn to **241**. If you fail, turn to **362**.

373

This vile repellent sight has cost you 2 points of Endurance. You and Harold stand in the middle of the great hall, while the creatures swarm over the machinery, seeking to surround you. How can you survive this horde? You will need some weapon suitable for mass combat.

Harold Lathers shouts, 'Quick! On the shelf is a weapon Ausbach uses upon those pets who displease him.'

Will you heed Harold's advice? Turn to **346**. Or will you grab one of the medieval weapons from the wall to your left? Turn to **148**.

374

A cavern stretches out before you, its floor littered with hundreds of clay models. Scorpions, crabs, beetles and other creatures vie for your attention – a pandemonium of insects and crustacea. Some are life size, but others are huge. In the lamplight their legs and bodies cast disturbing shadows, that seem to move as you thread your way across the cavern.

At first, apart from your footsteps, the cavern is silent. Then a tapping noise begins to reach your ears. You stop beside a giant model of a scarab beetle and listen. The noise is drawing nearer! Raising the lantern, you peer into the shadows.

Looming out of the darkness comes a giant red scorpion. It stands as high as your waist and menaces you with enormous claws. Worse still, you spot its sting, arched menacingly over the creature's ribbed body. Roll against your Mentality. If you succeed, turn to **359**. If you fail, turn to **292**.

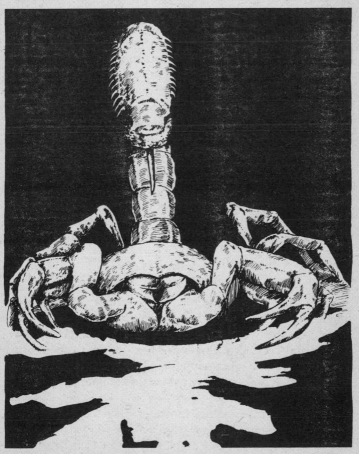

*375

You awake to find Petrie-Smith leaning over you, dabbing at your forehead with a damp cloth. You can remember little of your escape from the pyramid, beyond finding yourself once more in the room that lies at the edge of the underworld and fleeing through pitch-black corridors as they crumbled and shook around you.

Petrie-Smith tells you to rest and relates how he mustered a search party to hunt for you when the pyramid began to collapse.

'It was Harold who found you, slumped on the floor of the Grand Gallery. He says you were clutching this curious statuette.'

Your old friend passes you a crude representation of the god Thoth. In one hand he holds a mace and, in the other, the unmistakable figure of Baron Ausbach.

This ends the adventure, **Terrors out of Time.**

Improving your attributes

As you have succeeded in completing **Terrors out of Time**, you have earned the chance to improve your Strength, Dexterity and Mentality, in preparation for your next adventure.

Below, you will find a table with six columns and six rows. This table has positive numbers (representing improvements), negative numbers (representing reductions) and dashes (which indicate that no change has occurred to whichever attribute you are rolling for).

You may roll once on the table for each of the following attributes; Strength, Dexterity and Mentality. Whether you roll at all, or for only one or two attributes, is entirely up to you. But, if you do roll, you must apply the result, even if it is unfavourable. It should be noted that, if your Strength or Mentality is altered, this change will also affect your Stamina or Endurance by twice as much in the same direction. For example, if your Mentality rises by two, then your Endurance will rise by four.

Warning! The rules limit the maximum size of your Strength, Dexterity, and Mentality to nine points each. Therefore, if any of these attributes are already at nine, there is no point in rolling for them, unless you wish to risk reducing them! Similarly, if you have eight points in an attribute and gain a +2 you can only gain one point, as otherwise you would exceed the maximum allowed.

To use the table, roll one six-sided die and the score will tell you which column to look at. Then roll another die to discover which row you should use. Finally cross-index the row and column to discover the result. For example, you are rolling to improve your Strength. The first roll is a six and the second roll is a four.

Cross-indexing these rolls gives a +1. So your Strength will rise by one and your Stamina by two points.

If you gain a plus, it means the rigours of **Terrors out of Time** have helped to strengthen you for the encounters to come. If you suffer a loss, it means that, even though you managed ultimately to triumph, your experiences have damaged your health.

First die roll

		1	2	3	4	5	6
Second die roll	1	−1	−	+1	−	−	+1
	2	−	−1	−	−	−	−
	3	−1	−	−	−1	+1	−
	4	−	−	+1	−	−	+1
	5	−	−	+1	−	+1	−
	6	−1	−	−	−1	−	+2